LASSITER [illegible] OSS THE STR[illegible] ..

Lassiter said, "I want my gun."

"Don't know what the hell you're talking about," he snarled. He started to step away, but Lassiter blocked him.

"You took my gun. I want it."

Drinkers had come out of the saloon to stare at them.

"You're crazy as hell," the man blustered. "I never took no gun."

Lassiter's eyes finally lowered to the man's holster. He saw a familiar gun butt with black grips protruding from the leather.

"It's a good gun," Lassiter went on. "You must think it is too. You're wearing it."

The man looked at him for a moment, then his thick lips stretched tight in a grin. "Try an' take it…"

That was as far as he got. The .45 Lassiter borrowed appeared in his hand, the hammer eared back. The man came to his toes, a look of surprise on the brutal face.

"Don't bother to hand it over," Lassiter said softly. "I'll just take it…."

Other *Leisure* books by Loren Zane Grey:

LASSITER GOLD
A GRAVE FOR LASSITER
AMBUSH FOR LASSITER
LASSITER

LASSITER TOUGH

LOREN ZANE GREY

LEISURE BOOKS  NEW YORK CITY

A LEISURE BOOK®

August 2007

Published by special arrangement with Golden West Literary Agency.

Dorchester Publishing Co., Inc.
200 Madison Avenue
New York, NY 10016

ISBN: 0-8439-5817-0
ISBN 13: 978-0-8439-5817-1

Printed in the United States of America.

LASSITER TOUGH

1

Twice in one week Lassiter had been recognized in unlikely places. Once in New Mexico, with tragic results. And now here, deep in the Texas brush country, the brasada, a bearded stranger was calling out his name. The man had just entered O'Leary's Saloon, where Lassiter stood alone at the far end of the long and nearly deserted bar. Lassiter had been sipping whiskey while reflecting on the end of his search for a killer, which he felt was near. He was bone-weary, thinned down from the long, fast ride from New Mexico.

Upon entering the saloon, the big stranger had started toward a small group of men at the other end of the bar. Then he saw Lassiter standing alone.

"You're Lassiter," the man said in a low voice. The barkeep was reading a newspaper near the five other drinkers. A spring rain had been falling and the windows of the saloon that overlooked the business district of Santos were streaked.

"Yeah, I'm Lassiter." His nerves were tight because, so far as he was concerned, this was enemy territory.

"I seen you in action once. The day you stood up to Doc Kelmmer."

"*That* day."

"You got to admit Kelmmer was damn good. But you outdrew him."

"He called me. I had no choice."

"But you got him. That's the main thing. I never seen anything so fast in my life."

"Another minute and you'll turn my head with flattery," Lassiter said with a hard smile. He wondered where this was leading, but decided to keep his mouth shut and wait. There were too many loose ends here in the brasada for a mistake to be made.

"The minute I seen you standin' there, I says to myself, now there's the man for me."

Lassiter watched the man fetch paper and pencil from a pocket of his brush jacket and write on it. The man pushed the small piece of paper across the bar under Lassiter's nose. "Here's three names," he said.

"What about 'em?" Lassiter looked into the man's eyes, a peculiar shade of gray. They were fringed with reddish lashes. His eyebrows were the same color, coarse and tangled. What could be seen of his mouth through his reddish beard was thinned down, as if it had tasted mostly bitterness.

"I want 'em dead," the stranger said softly, pointing at the three names.

"I'm not a murderer." Unlighted brass lamps dangled from rough-cut ceiling beams on rusted chains. Yesterday the town had been full, the rotund barkeep had confided when Lassiter ordered his whiskey. But roundup was getting closer by the hour and men had left to prepare for it—a fact Lassiter well knew. He had been offered a job as ramrod here in the brasada, a job that had formerly been held by his late friend, his murdered friend.

"I want you to meet these three hombres like you done Kelmmer," the stranger said quietly, indicating the names he had written, Kilhaven, Rooney and Tate. "But meet 'em one at a time, of course." The man gave a hard laugh. "Don't reckon even Lassiter is good enough to face down three men at one time. Or maybe you are."

Lassiter tossed down the last of his drink and turned to go. But the man laid a strong hand on his arm. It caused Lassiter's eyes to suddenly turn cold as blue ice in a face that was long, darkened from years of sun. He had a wide mouth below a strong nose. He was one inch under six feet, with strong shoulders and long, powerful legs. Gently, he reached out and removed the stranger's hand from his arm.

"I'm willin' to pay for what I want done," the man went on in a low voice. "Three thousand. More'n you can make most weeks."

"No," Lassiter said.

The stranger's gray eyes showed displeasure. "I want you to meet 'em in a fair fight," he persisted, "before witnesses. A man like you can figure out some excuse to get 'em to face up to you."

"I'm not your man."

The stranger's large teeth showed through his beard. "I know, you're waitin' for me to up the ante. An' I guess maybe you're right. A job like I want done don't come cheap. I'll pay four thousand. Not a nickel more. What do you say to that, Lassiter?"

"I'm not interested." And if I did agree, Lassiter thought, you'd figure some way to get your money back.

"Damn it, a man like you? Hell, I heard you'll do anything for money."

"You heard wrong."

Again Lassiter started away. The stranger put out a restraining hand. But this time there was pressure in the fingers that gripped Lassiter's upper arm.

"Take your hand off," Lassiter warned coldly. Or they'll be sweeping your teeth off the floor, he thought, but he didn't say it. His eyes spoke for him.

The man straightened up, releasing Lassiter's arm. He was taller, heavier through the shoulders. At the far end of the big room a giant of a man stepped away from the other four drinkers. He stood with his thumbs hooked in a shell belt, a hat on the back of his round skull.

"Everything all right up there, Brad?" he called.

"Yeah," Brad said with a harsh laugh. "For now." Then he leaned close to Lassiter. "I ask you once more. Take my deal."

"Sorry." Lassiter wasn't sorry. It was just a handy word. But the man wasn't through. He tried twice more, then gave up.

"If you figure to tell anybody about the proposition I made you, I'll deny everything," the man said through his teeth. "Who you reckon they'll believe around here? You or me?"

At which point the man gave his full name, as if to impress Lassiter. It did, but not in the way the man thought.

Lassiter's shoulders stiffened under a black wool shirt and for just a moment anger altered his features. He smoothed them out. The man gave him a hard stare.

"You acted like you got somethin' against me all of a sudden!"

I heard your name. That was enough.

"I hadn't made up my mind about Rep Chandler's job as his ramrod," Lassiter said, hardly able to contain his rage. "Now I think I'll take it."

He threw a coin on the bar that rattled in the stillness. He took his time walking out of the saloon.

Lassiter felt the eyes of the seven men, including the barkeep, drilling his back. He got his horse from the hitching post, mounted, and turned east in the direction of Rep Chandler's Box C Ranch. It was a street lined with adobe and frame buildings, all showing age, some from a time when Texas had been ruled by Mexico.

His heart pounded with cold excitement as he repeated the name of the stranger through his mind again and again. Although he had been debating whether or not to take the job Chandler offered, now his mind was made up. He looked forward to settling the score for his dead friend, a very good friend.

It had stopped raining and the sun was out. He thought back on the proposition that had been put to him in O'Leary's Saloon. The arrogant bastard wanted to eliminate three men whose names were written in pencil on a scrap of paper, wanting someone to blame, once the job was done. Who else but Lassiter? No thanks.

Dogs sought spring noonday shade under wagons, the pups springing to chase occasional bits of paper blowing along the rutted street. In a blacksmith shop smelling of charcoal and hot metal, a smithy sang in a rich baritone as he hammered a muleshoe into shape. He paused to wipe his face as Lassiter rode past. The perspiring man stared at the lean figure astride a black horse, noting aquiline features somewhat spoiled by a beaklike nose. The man rode with the grace of a Comanche warrior. When he saw the gun in the low-cut holster, a little shiver ran down his back.

As Lassiter rode out, two men were summoned from the group of five drinking at the end of the bar in O'Leary's. One of them was the big man, Shorty Doane, the other Doug Krinkle, with a narrow, heavily freckled face.

"Doug, you an' Shorty teach that bastard a good lesson," said the bearded man. "Says he aims to work for Chandler. I say no."

"They'll have to ship that hombre outta Texas on a stretcher, Brad," Doane said with a grin and clenched oversized fists.

"Or in a pine box," Krinkle laughed and took a hitch at his gun belt.

When the two men left the saloon, Lassiter was already far down the road that threaded its way through walls of brush high as a rider.

2

Exactly one week prior to his arrival in Texas, Lassiter was ending a long ride, all the way down from the Mogollons. That day he had been ready for a bottle, a meal and whatever delights the border town of Ardon, New Mexico, might offer. But from the looks of it, huddled at the foot of bleak hills in the last light of what had been a trying day, he didn't have much hope.

He was just instructing a stable hand in the care of his weary black horse when a man came running across a weed-grown lot, shouting his name.

Lassiter turned to stare at the man through the wide stable doorway. The stranger was possibly fifty and lank as a ridge pole, his beard and hat brim blowing in a brisk wind.

"Lassiter, Lassiter . . ." He came up, panting, to stare into Lassiter's dark face. "You are Lassiter, ain't you?"

Ever on guard for tricks, Lassiter glanced at the far edge of the weedy lot where the man had first appeared. But he saw nothing suspicious in a few scraggly cottonwoods between the stable and an adobe house. Tree limbs stirred in the wind.

"Why you want to know about Lassiter?" he demanded.

"Fella . . . young fella over yonder . . ." The stranger, so out of breath he could hardly speak, jerked a bony thumb in the direction of the adobe house that could barely be seen through the screen of trees. "Bad shot, he is. He seen you ride in an' he asked me to fetch you. If you really are Lassiter, that is. He only had a glimpse of you. . . ."

Lassiter sniffed for a possible trap. Over the years he had accumulated a fair share of enemies and was taking no chances. "What young fella you talking about?" he asked sharply, wondering who could know him in this forlorn end of nowhere.

"Name of Tevis. I think that's what he said. Vince Tevis. Him an' the gal just got in town about an hour ago. . . ."

"I know a Vince Tevis." Lassiter remembered an amiable drifter. Vince, son of Ralph Tevis, had befriended a lonely Lassiter when he was a boy. A strong tie had endured over the years, even after the elder Tevis had died. The last letter Lassiter had received from Vince said he was working in the Texas brush country. It was over a year ago and at the moment Lassiter couldn't recall the name of the outfit.

"You say he's been shot?" Lassiter demanded.

"Bad." The man, who said he was Ben Sampson, was recovering his breath. But Lassiter still wasn't sure. Sampson was saying, "I'd just showed him an' the gal where they could sleep in the old Ortiz 'dobe an' right after that them fellas come along an' kicked the door in. They shot Tevis an' run off with the gal. . . ."

"Didn't anybody go after 'em?"

"Nobody left in this town who'll try an' run down tough hombres like them three."

Lassiter made up his mind. He wheeled to the wide-eyed hostler who was standing a few feet away in the cavernous stable that had only three filled stalls. He was holding the reins of Lassiter's black horse. "I heard the gunshot, I did," the man said.

"Hold up on doing anything for my horse till I get back!" Lassiter snapped. Then, taking Sampson by the shoulder, he pushed him toward the doorway. "You go ahead of me," he ordered.

"Hell, it ain't no trick, if that's what you're thinkin'."

"One way I've lived this long is because I always make sure."

Sampson was at a stumbling run across the vacant lot, a tense Lassiter at his heels. With their clothes flapping in the wind, Lassiter pounded through the cottonwoods and reached the adobe. Seen up close, it was little more than a shack. Boards had replaced glass at one of the windows. The front door was splintered. If Sampson could be believed, heavy boots had kicked it in.

When Sampson hesitated at the doorway, Lassiter gave him a shove. "Go on in. I'll follow."

"Them fellas might come back," Sampson said fearfully, glancing up and down the deserted street. A block away, a window glowed with early lamplight that touched a sign: CANTINA. "You still in there, Tevis?" Sampson called nervously into the shadowed house.

"Did . . . did you get . . . get Lassiter?"

Lassiter recognized the voice, weak as it was. In the shadows he saw a man lying on a pallet that rested on a floor of tamped-down earth. Across the room a bed with rumpled blankets held some articles of feminine apparel. He could barely make out a camisole, petticoat and gray dress.

Lassiter dropped to one knee beside the pallet on the dirt floor. The pallet was deeply stained with blood. He had a vague impression of Vince's face in the shadows. He asked Sampson to fetch a lamp, which he did. Tevis was speaking haltingly.

"You an' me . . . last time we worked together . . . XK outfit. Arizona."

"I remember, Vince." A match scratched. Lamplight flooded the small room. Lassiter took the lamp from Sampson and set it on the floor. Despite his obvious agony, Tevis was still rather handsome, not having aged much in the three years since Lassiter had last seen him. He was holding one hand to the front of a bloodied shirt.

"She's a nice kid," Tevis gasped, reaching out to grip Lassiter's arm. He was rambling. "I . . . I tried to help her . . . been tryin' to find her aunt, we was. But . . . but the bastards finally caught up with us here. . . ."

Lassiter barked orders to Sampson who was looking on with a worried expression on his wrinkled face. "Go fetch some arnica and laudanum and clean cloths. And a bottle of whiskey!"

Sampson scampered away, starting at a run across vacant lots toward the cantina in the next block.

Tevis increased the pressure of his fingers on Lassiter's arm. His amber eyes were wide, staring. A droplet of blood appeared at a corner of his mouth, then rolled down his chin.

"Let me have a look at your chest," Lassiter said with concern.

"Find her, Lassiter . . . she's a good kid an' she don't deserve . . ." The voice trailed away.

"Who is she, Vince?" Lassiter was remembering that his old friend's amorous pursuits had sometimes led to difficulties. Was this one of the same? To end tragically? Lassiter's breath caught at the thought.

Tevis had to pause for breath as Lassiter fumbled for buttons on the front of the blood-soaked shirt. "He's been trackin' us from the start," Tevis gasped. "The bastard. He . . . he stole her. . . ."

"Give me a name, Vince. A *name*. Who stole her?"

"Sanlee," Tevis whispered.

Because the man's voice had sunk so low, Lassiter wasn't sure if he had heard the name correctly. "Sam Lee? You say his name is Sam Lee?"

Tevis continued to stare up into Lassiter's face, the light in his eyes fading fast. His fingers suddenly fell away from Lassiter's arm and his head dropped back.

"Hang on, Vince!" Lassiter urged. But the man was past the point of clinging to life. Lassiter felt for a pulse, but it was useless. Mingled sadness and anger toward the perpetrators of this lethal act turned him cold.

All he had to go on was a name—Sam Lee.

By now it was almost fully dark. The wind continued to whip through the open door, causing the lamp on the floor to flicker.

Just as Lassiter sank back on his heels, preparing

to rise, he heard rapid footsteps above the howl of wind. From the sounds, it seemed two men were approaching the house from the side where the window was boarded up. There were no sounds of heels striking the hard ground, however, only the soft forepart of boots. Men running lightly on tiptoe to minimize the sound of their approach.

Just as Lassiter slapped a hand to his holstered .44, a gun crashed. The lamp exploded. In that moment, Lassiter noticed two shadowy figures crouched just beyond the doorway.

Instinctively, in the flash of gunfire, he rolled away from the shattered lamp and across the hard-packed floor. He was lifting his gun, preparing to sit up, when two more shots winked orange-red in the thickening darkness. Bullets cut long grooves into the dirt floor next to Lassiter's cheek. A gout of blinding dirt struck his eyes. But even gripped by blindness, he still had the images and positions of the crouched gunmen locked in his mind. When he snapped off two quick shots, he heard a muffled groan of pain from one man, then a scream from the second.

As Lassiter rubbed at his stinging eyes, he heard one of them getting away, at a lurching run from the sounds he made. Low moans at each labored step began to rapidly diminish. In a few moments there were hoofbeats, heading in an easterly direction. They were fading fast.

Although one of them was making a break for it, there was no sound from the other man. Desperately, Lassiter pulled a bandanna from his hip pocket and tried to wipe dirt from his eyes. It restored only partial vision, so that he was forced to hold his head far back to even see at all through slitted lids. Gripping his gun, he slowly got to his feet. He had a distorted view of a huddled figure, wind whipping at the clothes, which lay just beyond the doorway. Sounds of the horse ridden by the fleeing second man were almost inaudible by then above the whistling wind.

Still barely able to see, and with his eyes smarting, Lassiter thumbed a match alight in order to see the face of the man he had shot. He lay on his side, a brutal nature revealed in pale eyes and the cruel twist of lips in a high-cheekboned face. Although the bullet had made only a small indentation just above the bridge of his nose, it had taken out a good portion of the rear skull in its exit. Some three feet away, a small puddle of blood was rapidly sinking into the dry ground, no doubt from the second man. And beyond it were footprints and traces of blood. The second man was apparently badly wounded.

Lassiter, so gripped by the pain of his eyes and knowing he was vulnerable in the doorway, allowed the still-burning match to sear his fingertips. He dropped it, swearing an oath. Then, with blurred vision, he saw about a half-dozen men watching him in the last of the twilight. One of them was Sampson, who held a bottle of whiskey and a small package.

"I . . . I got what you wanted, Lassiter," he called in a weak and frightened voice. "But what *happened?*"

"One of 'em is getting away," Lassiter shouted in his frustration. "Isn't there an ounce of guts in this town so some of you would get after him?"

The men shifted their feet but didn't answer. With his eyes still burning and open to mere slits, Lassiter groped his way toward the lighted window of the cantina.

Two Mexicans were drinking beer at the bar. They

turned to stare at Lassiter, kicking his way through sawdust on the floor. The barkeep was also Mexican, with big arms and a scowling face. A dark-eyed girl in a dress trimmed in red was strumming a guitar. But she broke off on a discordant note. No one spoke.

"I need water to wash out my eyes," Lassiter said, squinting. "And a drink." When they only stared at him, he repeated it in Spanish.

The barkeep nodded his head and told the girl to get water. Then he set out a bottle and glass. "It shows you have been around my people much," he said to Lassiter. "You speak my language well."

Lassiter realized then that he still held his gun. No wonder they had been silent and apprehensive. He let the weapon slide into its oiled holster. Then, his eyes watering, he poured himself a drink. It was liquid fire that seared throat and belly, but most welcome.

The girl brought a pitcher of water, a pan and clean cloths. Gingerly, he went about washing out his eyes. Within ten minutes, sips of whiskey in between, his vision had been nearly restored.

The bartender, whose name was Miguel Sandoval, answered his question. No, he had never heard of anyone named Sam Lee.

Sandoval said the man and the young woman had come into town on the stagecoach that ran only once a week since the mines had closed down and the town was practically deserted. He said the girl seemed to be either ill or frightened. She had done a lot of screaming. Sandoval had seen her only from a distance. She and Tevis had barely gotten settled in the old Ortiz adobe when there was a gunshot. And Sandoval saw one of the three men ride off with the girl. Two of them stayed behind, probably intending to finish off the man Tevis in the adobe when it got dark.

"Isn't there any law in this town?" Lassiter asked bitterly. "A man is shot and nobody does a damn thing about it."

Sandoval gave him a patient smile. "There is no law. And here, amigo, we have had too many years of guns and blood. We mind our own business."

An old story in the West, Lassiter well knew. Never had he felt more frustrated. His eyes still burned. But that was not the only reason he was out of sorts. It was because his old friend Vince Tevis was dead. And there had been the later attempt on his own life. Besides that, a young girl had been kidnapped. And no one in this wart on the face of God's green earth had tried to avenge either Tevis or the girl.

A thin smile touched Miguel Sandoval's lips. "My guess is her husband, he come to take home his runaway wife."

The possibility had also occurred to Lassiter. "One of the men who stayed behind was big and tough-looking," Lassiter said, mentioning the one he had killed. "What'd the other two look like?"

"The one who took the girl was big also. That's all I see because he ride away fast. The other one was tall as you. Tejanos."

"How do you know they're Texans?"

"Them two, the one you kill an' the other one, they come in for drinks after the shooting."

Lassiter drew a deep breath. "Then this Sam Lee is probably the same Texas breed," he mused aloud.

"Texas not too far," the Mexican said, waving a hand toward the east and south—the direction taken by the horse of the wounded man.

Lassiter left five dollars with Miguel Sandoval to pay for a gravedigger for Vince Tevis, then started out. By moonlight, he picked up the bloodied trail without too much trouble and followed it most of the night. But the following day the blood on the trail was gone. However, the tracks he had been following continued. The fleeing man had evidently taken time during the night to bind up his wound, Lassiter reasoned, hence the lack of blood. The tracks were fairly easy to follow because the shoe on the right forefoot was an odd shape, slightly different from the other three and made a deeper indentation whenever there was loose ground.

He gave the rising sun a hard smile and made a vow to continue the hunt.

No matter how far the unknown, wounded Tejano might ride, Lassiter would eventually run him to ground, him and the mysterious Sam Lee. He owed it to Vince Tevis, who had been his friend, and to the memory of the kindly father. Even though Vince had been a free spender and usually broke, Lassiter liked him. A ladies' man and evidently still retaining his touch clear to the end.

Yes, he owed it to Vince Tevis, but also to the unknown young woman, fleeing wife or not, who quite possibly had been trying to escape a brutal husband, basing his evaluation on the two remaining Texans, the wounded one and Sam Lee. They were undoubtedly of the same stripe as the man he had killed; never had he seen a more arrogant and brutal face even in death.

In the passing days, Lassiter followed the trail until his luck ran out. A heavy rainstorm in this early spring obliterated the tracks he was following. And although he failed to pick them up again, he pressed onward. For now he was in the Texas brasada, the thorny brush country that was hell on man and beast. It was from here that Vince Tevis had written him last, over a year ago, the letter finally catching up to him. Instinctively, he sensed that here in this brush country he would be settling the score for Tevis and the unknown girl. And here he would find Sam Lee.

And one day, as he rode deeper into the brush, the name of the outfit Tevis had worked for suddenly came to him. The Box C, owned by a man named Chandler.

Since the shooting back in New Mexico, the brand and owner's name had been blanked out of his mind. But it was as if thick storm clouds had rolled aside and there, in blinding sunlight, he saw it plainly in letters of fire.

He smiled grimly to himself.

3

He located Chandler, a lean, stooped man with a thick mustache that drooped over the corners of his mouth. A splinted-and-bandaged right leg rested on the seat of a straight-backed chair. He was sitting on the veranda of a rambling adobe ranch house.

When Lassiter introduced himself, Chandler looked at him more closely. "Be damned. Vince talked a lot about you."

"Vince worked for you, didn't he?"

"Yeah. An' he run out on me right when I busted my leg. Never said a word. Only a note sayin' somethin' come up an' he had to leave. Was figurin' on him for roundup, me bein' outta it on account of my leg. You know what happened to him?"

"He's dead."

Chandler was silent for several moments while staring off across the brushy flats that seemed to stretch to infinity. "Dead. Well, I'll be damned." He turned to stare at Lassiter, who leaned back against the porch rail. "Maybe it's the Lord slippin' Tevis a bad hand from the deck for runnin' out on me. Where'd he get killed?"

"Over north and west." Lassiter nodded in that direction. He wasn't inclined at this point to give details, not until he learned a few facts. "You know a man named Lee?"

"Lee what?" Chandler asked, looking up.

"It's his last name. First name's Sam."

"Sam Lee?" Chandler mused. Then his face changed and he added carefully, "Don't reckon I do."

Was there a sudden wariness in Chandler's light brown eyes? Lassiter wondered. Or was it his imagination? Some of Chandler's vaqueros were riding in, laughing among themselves. They dismounted down by the corral and started to unsaddle.

Chandler seemed deep in thought. Then he said, "Tevis said you was a good man, Lassiter. A good roper an' mighty handy with a gun. I could sure use you. Roundup starts in three days. . . ."

"I've got things to do before I can make up my mind about *anything*," Lassiter put in quickly.

But Chandler seemed desperate to have Lassiter accept the job of bossing his roundup crew. He asked Lassiter to stay and they'd discuss it over whiskey, even told him where a bottle and glasses could be found in the parlor. It would save him limping into the house on the bad leg, Chandler explained. Chandler became almost tearful in his entreaties as Lassiter kept backing off. Chandler said he'd prayed to the good Lord to send him somebody and then out of nowhere Lassiter had appeared.

"Do it in memory of Vince Tevis," Chandler urged, "if it ain't for the money. 'Cause I'll pay you damn good."

"We'll see," Lassiter said at last. The job Chandler outlined was tempting. He had nothing to tie him down at present. Once before, some years ago, he had worked a roundup in the Texas brush. It was an ultimate challenge for sure, because in all the West there was no more hazardous stretch of country than the brasada.

But first he had to hunt down the mysterious Sam Lee and make him pay up for complicity in the murder of Vince Tevis and the possible kidnapping of a girl.

He thought again about Chandler's reaction when he had mentioned Sam Lee. The rancher's eyes had lowered quickly. An involuntary show of surprise? It seemed so to Lassiter.

Somewhere he had lost the trail of the wounded man. But he had found the rancher who had hired Tevis as foreman. And it stood to reason that Sam Lee would be in the vicinity if Tevis had quit his job suddenly to run off with a girl. A girl that Sam Lee had trailed and finally captured.

Weary after the long ride from New Mexico, he needed a drink—alone—not with Chandler or anyone else. He needed time to start putting loose ends together.

So he rode a few miles to the town of Santos and entered O'Leary's Saloon. . . .

Doug Krinkle nodded at Lassiter riding fifty yards ahead on the brush-lined road. "There he is. Seems like we're s'posed to talk him outta workin' for Chandler," Krinkle said with a laugh.

"Yeah," Shorty Doane grunted. At six feet four and weighing two hundred and thirty-five pounds, his nickname, applied in jest some years before, had stuck. "Let's go get him."

Lassiter heard the two horses. He turned in the saddle and recognized the riders as having been in O'Leary's Saloon.

At first he thought they might be going to ride right on past him. But when they were abreast, they pulled up to match the stride of his horse. The slender, freckle-faced one was grinning on his right, the giant on the left.

Lassiter suddenly reined in his black horse. The pair, caught by surprise, rode on a few feet before halting. They looked back.

"If you hombres figure to keep me company," Lassiter said coldly, "I don't want any. Move along."

Shorty Doane laughed and rubbed the knuckles of a clenched right fist along the seam of his Levis. "Tough talk," he said to his companion.

"Brad Sanlee don't want you takin' that job with Rep Chandler," Krinkle said and lazily reached for his gun.

So that was it!

Hardly had the last word slipped through Krinkle's lips in his surprised face before Lassiter was ramming in the spurs. His black horse leaped before Krinkle finished speaking. It sideswiped Krinkle's dun with such force that the rider lost his seat. He went sailing off the horse, arms and legs beating the air.

So quickly had Lassiter moved that Shorty Doane wasted the time it took in forming a startled "O" with thick lips. Then he sent a hand streaking for his gun. But Lassiter had drawn his own weapon. He was turning the lunging black horse so as to enable him to reach the left side of Shorty Doane's broad skull with the barrel of his .44. Doane went backwards off the rump of his horse. He lay flat on his back in the Texas mud, arms and legs wide from his oversized body, a startled look on his scarred face. A few feet away, Krinkle, in fetal position, was beginning to stir.

Lassiter disarmed both men before they could fully recover consciousness. Krinkle was staring up at him out of dazed eyes. Doane had an ugly gash on the left side of his skull. Blood trickled into his ear and to the muddy road, making a small puddle.

Angrily, Lassiter unloaded rifles and revolvers belonging to the pair. He hurled cartridges into the thick brush on one side of the road and the weapons, one by one, far out into the thorny Texas jungle.

"Tell Brad Sanlee," he said to the dazed Krinkle, "that I'll be seeing him."

It was the name the arrogant bastard in the saloon had uttered to impress him. Not Sam Lee. Vince Tevis, who had been in great pain at the time, had mumbled a name that Lassiter had simply misunderstood. Sanlee.

Just as Lassiter mounted up, something made him look over his shoulder. A beautiful blonde on a bay mare, unnoticed till now, was watching him forty feet or so down the road. She wore a green silk blouse that fit snugly across full breasts, and a leather-divided riding skirt. Her red lips were parted in surprise.

Lassiter tensed as she urged her bay forward a few feet. She sat in her saddle, looking down at Krinkle, who was sitting up, holding his head, and at Doane, now blinking his eyes.

"So Sanlee sent his skullbusters after you," she

said in a deeply sensuous voice. Her eyes, a startling green, settled on his face. She wore a faint smile. "It seems they lost."

Then she sank in the spurs and rode quickly in the direction of town. She was laughing so hard that tears came to her lovely eyes. . . .

4

At a bend in the road, the beautiful woman looked back and saw the dark stranger heading east. Why hadn't she at least asked his name? There had been something fascinating about him. The penetrating blue eyes when he stared at her had put a hollow feeling in her stomach. Who was he? She had never seen him before.

She continued on to Santos, aware that her heart was acting strangely. She was Isobel Hartney and owned the Hartney Store in Santos, which had been started by her grandfather. She had been East, attending an academy for young ladies, when news reached her that Jonas Hartney, her father, had died suddenly. It gave her an excuse to cut short her education and hurry back to Texas to run the store.

Witnessing the stranger manhandle Krinkle and Doane had been a delight. Maybe Brad wouldn't be quite so cocky as he'd become these last months since the passing of the autocratic Sanlee senior. Two weeks ago, or thereabouts, Brad Sanlee had gone riding off without a word to her. He had taken Ad Deverax and Rupe Bolin along. It was rumored that Brad had been in a rage that no one at his Diamond Eight seemed willing to discuss. One morning he had simply gone pounding off to the north with his two hardcases. Only Brad had returned. No one seemed to know what had happened to Deverax and Bolin. . . .

In O'Leary's Saloon, the identity of the stranger had been no secret to Brad Sanlee. He had recognized him instantly, standing tall and brooding at the far end of the bar. It had brought back memories of an exciting afternoon in Tucson some three years before where he had been on business for his father. He had seen Lassiter stand up to Doc Kelmmer. Kelmmer, with eight notches in his gun, had intended to add Lassiter's before the day was out. But it hadn't worked out that way.

And today Lassiter, damn him, had turned down a decent proposition cold, which Sanlee couldn't understand. After witnessing Lassiter blow two holes in Kelmmer quicker than a man can blink, Sanlee had heard talk from excited onlookers afterward. They had said that Lassiter was a cold-hearted killer who'd spit in the devil's eye if somebody paid him. Tough enough to stare down a rattlesnake, others had said. Well, today he had refused a fine offer of four thousand dollars—a sum that Sanlee had figured to get back one way or another, once Lassiter was no longer of any use to him. The fact that Lassiter had flung the proposition in his face had been insulting.

Here he'd had all those frustrating days up north trying to pick up the trail of a wayward female, finally locating her and bringing her screeching and clawing all the way home. And then today having had a brilliant idea, which would have made up for all the frustration, when he'd seen Lassiter in the saloon.

Lassiter didn't know it, but he was in for one hell of a big surprise down the east road. Sanlee grinned at the thought of Shorty using his fists. Lassiter would likely be in such bad shape he'd have to be carried out of Texas in a sack.

Sanlee gave a fierce grin to his three men who had remained in O'Leary's. "Drink up, you bastards. It's the last you'll git till roundup's over. Three weeks of pure hell in the Texas brush."

After another drink, he mused aloud, "Kind of a shame in a way. Lassiter was a legend. An' after today, it'll be the end of it. . . ."

He broke off. Through the front windows of the saloon, he saw Krinkle and Doane come riding in. Doane was leaning far over, the saddle horn punching his big belly. He was bare-headed and the side of his face was streaked with dried blood.

Krinkle didn't appear to be in much better shape. When he dismounted at the hitching post, his movements seemed to give him pain. He tried to help Doane out of the saddle, but the big man's weight was too much. They both sprawled to the boardwalk. Men came at a run.

"Go out an' give 'em a hand," Sanlee ordered his three riders. Then he poured himself another drink and stared moodily at his reflection in the mirror in back of the bar.

"Son of a bitch," he said suddenly. "Damn, if Lassiter ain't livin' up to his rep." Then he began to laugh, pounding the bar with his fist so that plump-and-balding Sid O'Leary looked around in surprise. "One way or another," Sanlee was saying, still howling with laughter, "I got to have that man in my hip pocket. He's one I can use, by God!"

A shame-faced and angry Krinkle finally related what had happened, with embellishments in their favor. Sanlee didn't believe him. Then Sanlee sent them down to Doc Clayburn's. Doane was still stretched out on the boardwalk and had to be helped.

An hour later, Lassiter was still angry at the attempt of the two Sanlee men to box him in. He thought about Sanlee. It was logical that the man Tevis had named with practically his last breath would come from the area where he had been working.

He could see the Chandler ranch house up ahead, the rain-washed, dun-colored walls shining in the sunlight. It was located on a large rise of ground for defensive purposes and commanded a view of the miles of brush on all sides. Brush had been hacked away near the house but it was a constant battle to keep it from overrunning everything.

Some of Chandler's vaqueros were by the bunkhouse. When Lassiter rode up, they grew quiet. The segundo, Luis Herrera, regarded him gravely. He was chunky with a rope of mustache that looked as if it had been fashioned from black silk. He and his wife, Esperanza, lived in a small house in some cottonwoods. When Lassiter dismounted, the vaqueros drifted away.

"I guess you decide to take the job, no?" Herrera said with a faint grin.

"You a mind reader, Luis?"

"You come back. If you make up your mind not to take it, you keep going."

"Something bothers me, Luis. You're already segundo. The next step up is foreman."

Herrera studied the pointed toe of his boot, which he dug into the mud. "I'm happy where I am."

"Did the old man ever ask you to take over?"

Herrera thought about it, then looked Lassiter in the eye. "He worries now about roundup. He hears you're a good man. He wants you to see him through."

Although Lassiter wasn't satisfied with the answer, he decided to accept it for the present. When he related the encounter with the pair of Sanlee men, whom he described, Herrera was impressed.

"A wonder Krinkle didn't shoot out your liver an' Doane bust your back in three places. Them's tough hombres." Then Herrera laughed. "You also a tough hombre, amigo."

Lassiter went up to the house to see Chandler. The rancher was sitting in his parlor, his splinted leg resting on a stool. His eyes, faded from years of squinting into the Texas sun, studied Lassiter as he whipped around a chair to straddle.

"Lassiter, you make up your mind yet?"

"Like Herrera said, if I decided not to take the job, I wouldn't have come back."

Chandler's seamed face broke into a smile. "That's damn good news, Lassiter." For a middle-aged rancher, incapacitated with a broken leg, he seemed unusually happy.

"Tell me something, Mr. Chandler . . ."

"Call me Rep. The only ones around here call me mister are my vaqueros."

"How about Herrera?"

"Well, he's a little different."

"How come you didn't make him foreman when Tevis left?"

Chandler studied a patch of cobweb on the ceiling. "Texas brush country is the toughest place on God's earth to hold a roundup. I wanted a man with experience."

"I'm sure Herrera has experience. . . ."

"You tryin' to talk yourself outta the job?" Chandler chuckled. "Let's have us a drink. Hurts me to move, so how about you fetchin' the bottle an' glasses?" He waved a long-fingered hand at a sideboard. "I tell you right off," Chandler said as they were drinking. "I'm thinkin' of askin' you to stay on full time after roundup."

"Well, now, I don't know. . . ."

"I heard somethin' today that kinda changes my plans." Chandler seemed elated about whatever it was he had heard.

"That so?" It was all Lassiter could think to say.

"Yep. Might be fixin' to get myself married."

"Congratulations." Lassiter took a swallow of the good whiskey. Across the room was a big stone fireplace and above it a pair of horns from a Chihuahua steer with the widest spread Lassiter had ever seen.

"I'll want me an' the new wife to do some pokin' around this ol' world. I done real well since the war an' I figure to spend some of the money I made pushin' cows up to Kansas."

"The lucky lady a local girl?"

Chandler, still smiling, looked mysterious. "Best I don't talk no more about it till I do some dickerin'."

Lassiter finished his drink, wondering if Chandler's reference to dickering meant the dowry of his bride-to-be.

He switched the subject to his encounter with Brad Sanlee and later with his two men. Then he mentioned the three names on Sanlee's list that he wanted eliminated.

When Lassiter finished, Chandler sat staring down at a bead of whiskey that remained in the bottom of his glass. Then he drained it and said, "Brad was just joshin' with you. Hell, they're all good neighbors of mine an' his. All good friends we are, mighty good."

Lassiter got to his feet and put the empty glass on a table that bore a daguerreotype of a round-faced woman in a high-lace collar. "Sanlee offered me three thousand for the job at first. Then he raised it another thousand."

"Brad's mighty close with a dollar. Learned it from his pa who'd beat the bejeezus outta him if he spent more'n he should. Brad was just havin' fun with you today."

But Lassiter knew otherwise and sensed Chandler did also.

Then Chandler said with forced joviality, "Brad'll be some put out that you busted up his two men. But it'll make him understand you're nobody to fool with."

But Sanlee already knew that, Lassiter reflected, having witnessed him gun down a no-good braggart named Doc Kelmmer, a man wanted by half the sheriffs of the West.

Chandler's pale eyes narrowed. "You come here lookin' for somebody named Sam Lee, so you told me. Well, I figured you meant Sanlee, but I couldn't figure out why you was so interested. Mind tellin' me about it?"

"I heard the name is all." This was more or less the truth. "But I got it all wrong." He decided to say no more, not even about the girl's part in it. He'd let everything unfold in natural order.

Chandler insisted on them having another drink, then talked about the cattle business.

"Reckon I'll get Herrera to show me where we'll be holding roundup," Lassiter said.

"Seems like every year one or the other of the outfits loses a man or two. If it ain't a man gettin' his throat tore out with thorns or a steer horn in the belly, he's liable to get kicked to death by a wild ladino. But you know all that anyhow. . . ."

"I worked roundup for Major Mitchell over east of here."

"I recollect you sayin' so, yes." Chandler rubbed his splints. "An' here I am laid low with this damn leg an' with roundup comin' on. An' me likely takin' a new wife." He waved toward the daguerreotype on the table. "That there's Bertha—been gone three years now. You reckon that's long enough to wait before takin' another wife?"

"Sure it is," Lassiter said. The big house smelled of dust and cobwebs and field mice. Chandler's new wife would have a cleaning job on her hands.

"Me takin' this certain gal as my bride will make things some different in this part of the country," Chandler mused.

Lassiter wondered in what way things would be different. But Chandler failed to explain. All Lassiter intended to do was to finally make Sanlee pay for his part in the murder of Vince Tevis and earn some money as Chandler's ramrod at the same time. Chandler had set his pay at a hundred a month, plus 10 percent of the gross from a cattle sale. No one could fault those terms. Chandler had done well in the cattle business and evidently didn't mind sharing it.

But why not share the good fortune with Luis Herrera? Lassiter wondered again. But he decided not to bring it up—at least for the present. He had a ranch to run which was trouble enough without mixing in sidelines, such as the segundo, or who Chandler might be taking as his bride. Some local widow, still personable and with a little money of her own, Lassiter assumed.

After going to the quarters assigned to him, Lassiter cleaned his .44 revolver and Henry rifle, to be ready for any eventuality. He was thinking of the hard-nosed bearded owner of Diamond Eight, Brad Sanlee.

5

Just before the start of roundup, Lassiter met the three men on Brad Sanlee's death list, all of them tough Texans. Marcus Kilhaven was a tall, raw-boned quiet man of thirty or so with a hand-busting grip. Buck Rooney was heavier, a man with a hearty laugh. He had lost his wife a year before. Jasper Tate, stocky and dark, was the only one of the three with a wife. Kilhaven, for one reason or other, had never married.

Brad Sanlee's was the last of the five outfits to show up at the agreed site for roundup. Sanlee gave Lassiter a spare nod. Krinkle muttered something and Shorty Doane glared. But neither man made a threatening move.

Sanlee seemed to find the whole thing amusing and later got Lassiter aside as his men were setting up camp, which was away from the others. "I sure was peeved at you, Lassiter, for talkin' up to me like you done that day in town. So I wanted to have a little fun. I sent Krinkle an' Doane to tame you down a bit. But seems you're the one done the tamin'." Sanlee bellowed with laughter and slapped himself on the knee. But the merriment failed to reach his slate-gray eyes.

"Also your idea of fun to write out those three names?" Lassiter asked quietly.

Sanlee managed to look blank. "Don't know what you're talkin' about. What three names?"

"You're not much of an actor," Lassiter said with a tight grin. "You wouldn't make a dime behind the footlights."

"Hey, I kinda like you, Lassiter," Sanlee boomed. He started to throw a heavy arm across Lassiter's shoulders. But Lassiter stepped aside. He knew that old trick, in case Sanlee was intending to use it—a pretense of friendship, then grabbing a man in a bear hug and holding him while someone like Krinkle or Doane beat him down to his socks.

"You ain't very friendly, though," Sanlee said with a short laugh. He stomped over to where his men were spreading their blanket rolls.

For the first time, Lassiter noticed a small tent set a little apart from the bedrolls that were strung out across the cleared stretch of ground chosen for the Diamond Eight campsite. But he didn't think much about it till later, for the next hectic day he was busy chasing steers from their sanctuaries in the brutal brush. And rousting cows who could be even deadlier than the males. Calves were torn from their mothers and dragged kicking and bawling to the branding fires. There one of the branders would apply the proper red-hot iron to tender hide and ownership established.

There were also mavericks to brand, full-grown cattle that somehow had escaped the branding iron in previous roundups. Over the days, the joint herd at the holding grounds gradually increased. At completion of roundup, cowhands would cut out cattle according to brand for the individual owners.

Sanlee had the most in his Diamond Eight; Chandler was next with his Box C. Then came Kilhaven, Tate and Rooney, much smaller so far as numbers of cattle went, but big enough when it came to acreage. The three of them controlled a great stretch of the brasada to the east of Chandler's Box C.

What surprised Lassiter was to learn one day that there was a female in camp. Rafael Alvarez, a Chandler vaquero new to the area, mentioned that he had glimpsed her. He winked and exaggeratedly rolled his eyes. They were taking a breather after chasing some big longhorns into the herd. They were standing in the sparse shade of a mesquite, passing a canteen, when Alvarez started to say more about the mysterious female. But Luis Herrera told him in crisp, border Spanish to *la boca cerrada,* "keep the mouth closed."

Lassiter wondered at the warning. But he couldn't get Herrera to explain.

Then it was back to the almost impenetrable brush.

Everywhere was chaos, great clouds of dust from the drying ground, men shouting, steers roaring. And the occasional terrible cry of pain from one of the horses that could freeze a man's guts. And at times a similar cry from a human. If the wound was not too serious, it was quickly bound. And the wounded man was back in the fray. If injuries were of a permanent nature, the man was paid off and sent on his way. A cruel custom, Lassiter thought, and learned that it had been started by Sanlee's late father. The other ranchers seemed to go along with whatever custom the elder Sanlee had set.

Lassiter got his first look at the captive woman when he was herding some unruly steers, wanting to get them to the holding grounds as soon as possible because he had no help. So he took a shortcut across the edge of the Diamond Eight camp. That was when he saw her sitting cross-legged on the ground in front of the small tent. She was brushing her long black hair. Upon seeing him so close, her spine stiffened and she dropped the brush and clamped both hands to her kneecaps. She was wearing a faded blue dress.

In what was left of the late-afternoon sun he saw her dark eyes fixed on him with startling intensity—eyes that reminded him of olives freshly fetched from a tub and still moist. They stared hard as if to impart a message, so it seemed to him. A plea for help? That was when he first got the impression she was being held captive.

But the steers demanded his attention and he was forced to move on.

This first week of roundup he heard low-voiced speculation about her, always from newcomers hired on for roundup. But none of the regulars would discuss her at all. However, there was speculation among the new men that she was Brad Sanlee's woman and he was keeping an eye on her during roundup.

The following day it rained. As Lassiter started his rope-spinning overhead to make a cast, his horse slipped in the mud. Lassiter was thrown heavily. But he was instantly on his feet, dancing away nimbly. However, his pinto, struggling to get up from the muddy ground, took a steer horn in the belly. Its awesome scream knifed through the roundup camps. Entrails of the animal lay steaming where it had fallen.

Lassiter spun from the advancing steer, but it suddenly veered and went ambling into the brush.

With a dry mouth, Lassiter shot the suffering horse through the head. After stripping off saddle and bridle and carrying his rifle, he walked back to camp for a fresh mount. He gave thanks that it wasn't his black horse in a crumpled heap back in the brush.

It was late in the day when Lassiter, mounted on a chestnut horse, saw some ropers nearby let a wild ladino get away. It went crashing through the brush and across the Diamond Eight camp, scattering pots and bedrolls, bumping against the chuck wagon. Lassiter, who was the nearest, went pounding after it. A perfect cast of his rope pinned the forelegs and dumped the great beast on its nose.

In his rampage, the bull had crushed the woman's tent. She stood now beside the crumpled canvas, her face white, hands clenched at her sides.

And in those moments when his horse was backing away, to drag the bellowing mountain of flesh away from the chaos it had caused, she was looking at him intently again. She seemed younger than he had thought at first. He saw her lips move in greatly exaggerated fashion. He had never practiced lip-reading, but there was no mistaking her silent message: *Help me! Please help me!*

But by then, some of the Diamond Eight riders had come up and were cursing the big bull for what he had done to their camp. Brad Sanlee cantered in, saw that Lassiter had the fifteen-hundred pound ladino in hand and gave a jerk of his head in approval.

"See you got the bastard!" Sanlee shouted with a great show of white teeth through his beard.

Lassiter gestured at the woman, really a girl, who stood trembling beside the mound of canvas. "She was likely scared half to death when he got loose," Lassiter said, wondering at the man's reaction.

Sanlee didn't even bother to look at her, but his eyes, with their peculiar shade of gray, seemed to darken. "She's used to trouble, that one." He spoke so coldly as if to imply she was a nonentity, not to be discussed.

Sanlee shouted at two of his men to straighten up the scattered bedrolls but made no mention of her tent. She had turned her back and was trying to straighten out the tangle of damp canvas. No one offered to give her a hand. Anger shot through Lassiter at such indifference—the reflection of the attitude of a tough crew to a tough ranch owner, Lassiter supposed. And although he felt at home around such men, one thing he could not tolerate was to see that toughness turned on the weak and defenseless, or to demean a woman as was the case at the Diamond Eight roundup camp.

By then the bull was on its feet. Some of the Diamond Eight riders were herding it in the direction of the holding ground.

Lassiter rewound his catch rope, hooked it over the saddle horn and dismounted. At the moment, he didn't give much of a damn who might be watching him, but he wasn't going to stand by and let her try to erect the fallen tent by herself. Night was coming on and she'd have no shelter.

She was pulling forlornly at the pile of canvas when he came up behind her.

"Canvas takes on a lot of weight when it's wet," he said, pushing her gently aside. "Let me."

Her dark eyes flashed to his face and she brushed aside a sheaf of black hair that had fallen across her cheek.

"You shouldn't," she whispered tensely, glancing at Sanlee's broad back just disappearing in the brush some distance away.

"You asked me for help," Lassiter reminded her as he lifted a ridge pole and the canvas.

"But I didn't," she protested.

"I read it plain as day. Please help me."

She shrugged and said, "Perhaps I did. I was upset." She stood aside, arms folded, her teeth clamped so that he could see the neat white row they made—not a smile, but a grimace.

Thirty yards away a gray-bearded man hunched over the cook fire was watching him intently. He was the only crew member in camp. Sanlee and the others had returned to the business of roundup.

It took some twisting and stretching, but finally Lassiter got the girl's tent smoothed out. Soon he was grunting as he lifted the ridge pole with the full weight of canvas on it. When he had the tent righted, he went around it hammering in stakes with a flat rock.

"Thank you," the girl said without looking at him. She dropped to her knees and crawled into the tent. She lowered the flaps for privacy.

Lassiter led his horse over to the cook fire. The gray-bearded man was stirring the contents of a pot simmering on the fire. He had picked up the pots and pans scattered about by the raging bull.

"First time I ever heard of a woman at roundup camp," Lassiter said tentatively.

The old man put down a large spoon. His eyes were bright in a seamed face. He jerked at the brim of an old slouch hat and peered into the pot of beans and beef. Then he threw a few sticks of wood on the fire, which instantly burst into flame. A fresh column of smoke was pumped into the sky where it flattened out under the overcast.

"Brad Sanlee seen what you done," the old man said, not looking up. "He won't like it worth a damn."

"Not even you figured to give her a hand with that tent."

"I lived as long as I have by knowin' which side of the creek to wet my feet in."

"Just who is she, anyway?"

The old man limped over to the chuck wagon as if to indicate he'd said all he intended to on the subject.

Lassiter looked back at the tent. There was no sign of the girl.

Then he was back at the holding grounds with its mass of cattle, the branding fires, the shouting amidst sounds of pain and rage from the animals. Although it seemed chaotic with men running about, calves squealing, it was organized. Every man knew his job and did it.

Soon most of Lassiter's slim crew were drifting in for the evening meal. Others were helping guard the herd to keep it from stampeding. With nearly four thousand head of nervous cattle, it would take only a minor disturbance to set them into a panic run.

As Lassiter slumped wearily to the ground, he thought of the girl. She was pretty enough even in an old shirt and boy's breeches, her attire for the day. What would she be like with her hair put up and wearing a clean dress? He thought about it. That she was Sanlee's prisoner, one way or another, was evident. He thought of the last war that had been fought to free slaves. Apparently, the message hadn't as yet reached Sanlee. Lassiter's mouth hardened as he recalled her strained face when mouthing her plea for help.

Suddenly, he was striding toward his horse.

"Time to eat, Lassiter," Luis Herrera called to him from the shadows.

"Be back in a few minutes."

Herrera gave a worried tug at his silky black mustache. "Where you headin', anyhow?" Herrera asked.

"Figure to borrow some coffee beans."

"Hell, we got plenty," Rudy Ruiz sang out, who doubled as a cook. But Lassiter was already riding away.

6

At the Diamond Eight camp, the men were in various positions on the ground, some sitting cross-legged, others leaning against tree trunks or a wheel of the chuck wagon. Each man had a tin plate of food in his lap.

An ominous silence fell over the crew as an angry Lassiter rode into camp. Doug Krinkle nudged Shorty Doane, who still wore a dirty bandage around the head Lassiter had struck with his gun barrel. They looked over at Brad Sanlee, who sat alone, wolfing food from a plate that rested on his uplifted knees.

Sanlee's large head came up at sight of Lassiter and his bearded jaws stopped chewing the tough beef.

Lassiter's glance at the tent was not lost on Sanlee. The flaps were still down. Lassiter wondered if she'd had anything to eat.

The old cook, Tim Marshal, had just finished ladling a plateful of beef and beans for himself. He sat down on the ground as Lassiter reined in nearby.

"You got an almighty nerve comin' over here like this," the old man hissed. "You lose somethin' over here today?"

"Came to borrow some coffee beans," Lassiter said roughly, his eyes still on Sanlee some distance away.

Instantly, Sanlee became the jovial ranch owner. He beamed across the shadowed camp at Lassiter. "How come your cook didn't come to do the borrowin'? A foreman sure don't do it, Lassiter. Mine sure wouldn't, if I had one. But maybe Rep Chandler hired himself a different breed. You think that might be it, Lassiter?" He grinned, his teeth gleaming through the beard. Some of his crew wore tense smiles. Others seemed uneasy. The agreement among the five ranchers for roundup was that there was to be no trouble of a personal nature for the duration. There was time enough to settle grievances afterward. Too much time had been lost in the past, too many men injured, to put up with violence any longer when they were working cattle. The agreement had been drawn up by Marcus Kilhaven and the others had signed it.

In the uncomfortable silence, Lassiter was sure he saw one of the tent flaps move slightly. Was he under observation by the dark-haired girl?

Brad Sanlee lounged on the ground some four feet from the front of the tent, his long legs now outstretched, his back resting against the trunk of a sturdy mesquite. Lassiter skirted the semicircle of cowhands. Their knives and forks scraping the tin plates was a dull metallic sound in the twilight. Some of them were slurping the last spoonful of watery beans. But all eyes were on Lassiter as he rode over to where Sanlee was eating. Lassiter dismounted.

"Rep Chandler hired himself a foreman," Lassiter

said quietly. "And I'm it. But I used the coffee beans as an excuse. I wanted to have a talk."

He dropped the reins of his horse on the damp ground, his gaze boring into the gray eyes across from him. He could end it now, call Sanlee on the death of Vince Tevis and get it over with. Or should he hold his cards close to the vest and play each hand as it was dealt? He decided on the latter choice.

With a fierce grin, Sanlee jerked his thumb over his shoulder at the tent. "You wanta know about *her*. That's why you come."

"You read my mind," Lassiter said.

"Ever hear what happened to the cat that was curious?"

Lassiter's smile was cold. "This is some different."

"You're a cool one, Lassiter." Sanlee gave a short laugh. "Guess I'll believe it next time somebody says you got ice water in your veins instead of hot blood."

"I've got a strong hunch she's being held here. 'Against her will' is the way it's usually put." There it was, more words than he had intended to use. But the whole damn thing was getting away from him—mistreatment of the girl and the cold-blooded killing of Vince Tevis cracked the dam of his resolve.

Sanlee seemed to think about it. He cocked his head at Lassiter, who stood a few feet away, hands at his sides, feet widespread, nothing to read on the dark features. Sanlee used the last biscuit to mop up what remained of his supper. His strong jaws chomped on stringy beef. Then he tossed his plate aside, where it lay shining dully in a clump of weeds. As he wiped his mouth with the back of the left hand, his right hand darted to his belt. The move was as quick as that of a striking rattler. He had a gun half-drawn, then noticed that Lassiter's .44 was already in hand. The metallic sound as it was cocked seemed almost as explosive in the silent camp as a thunderclap.

"I shoulda remembered you got speed along with your nerve." Sanlee chuckled as he let his gun slide back into the holster.

The nearest man, some thirty feet away, sat rigidly in the twilight, his mouth open. Beyond him the rest of the crew stared. The old cook, Tim Marshal, on hands and knees, was reaching out for a rifle on the ground.

Sanlee caught the movement from a corner of his eye. "Easy, Tim," he called over to the cook. "We got a sidewinder in camp. Let's step real careful."

The old man sank back to the ground and wrapped his bony arms around his knees.

"Put away your gun, Lassiter," Sanlee said jovially. "You pullin' it so free an' easy is liable one day to get you in a pile of trouble."

"Not so far." Lassiter holstered his .44. For a minute he had let his temper get away from him, but now it was checked once again. There would come a day when everything would fall into place. And he would know that it was time to settle everything with this hulking killer sitting hunched across from him in the deepening shadows.

Lassiter accepted Sanlee's invitation to "set an' talk." He sank to his knees in a position where he could keep an eye on the crew. There were scraping sounds of sand on tin as they cleaned their plates. But as they worked at the daily chore, their eyes flicked to Lassiter.

"Didn't Chandler tell you about that gal in the

tent?" Sanlee asked, that hard smile still on his bearded face.

"Haven't seen Rep since roundup started."

"Then I'll tell you." Sanlee's voice lowered so that not even the nearest man could have overheard. "Millie's my kid sister. You believe that?"

"If you say so."

"Since my pa's been gone, I done my damnedest to keep her in hand. Most of the time I do. But about three weeks ago she run off." Sanlee's voice hardened but he failed to notice the change that had come over Lassiter's face. "She run off with a no-good bastard. . . ." Sanlee didn't go on with it.

Lassiter, his heart hammering, vowed not to let himself come unraveled as memories of that tragic evening in New Mexico came flooding back.

"This fella she ran off with," Lassiter managed to say, "she figured to marry him?"

Sanlee looked up, his eyes ugly. "I got my own idea on who she's gonna marry. You understand, Lassiter?"

"Looks like she's got nothing to say about it."

"Not one damn solitary thing. I aim to look after my little sister an' see that she ties up with a solid citizen of Texas. Millie's gonna marry your boss."

"Rep Chandler?" Lassiter asked in genuine surprise. He was remembering how young the girl had seemed. At least he now knew her name. "Guess it's your business," he went on carefully, "but it seems to me kinda like tryin' to squeeze together May and December."

"She needs an older fella like Rep to tame her."

"I see. . . ."

"Once my sister an' Rep are harnessed, the two outfits will be one, you might say. His an' mine."

Lassiter couldn't help a short laugh. "So that's it. Use your sister to get your hands on Chandler's ranch."

Sanlee seemed to take no offense, and said, "Had the idea for quite a spell. Kinda took your breath away, eh?" the rancher said with sly amusement. He plucked a green weed and stuck a stem into a corner of his bearded mouth. "Women are bought an' sold the same as slaves. You understand, Lassiter?"

"Hardly."

"Well, let me explain. I got somethin' Rep Chandler wants. He wants a hot-blooded young female an' Millie's all of that from what I been hearin' since she was fourteen or thereabouts. An' Chandler's got somethin' I want. His ranch added to mine will give me a sizeable chunk of the brasada."

"That figures," Lassiter said evenly. "What if I told Rep of your plans?"

"Go ahead. His heart's pumpin' so hard for my little sister he wouldn't even hear you." Sanlee leaned forward. "That's why I got Millie out here where I can keep an eye on her. You understand?"

"You put it plain enough." Lassiter was barely able to conceal his contempt, his outright hatred because of what had happened to his friend up in New Mexico.

Lassiter got to his feet and Sanlee stood up, his big body unwinding slowly, taller than Lassiter by an inch or so. Old Tim Marshal had thrown fresh fuel on the cook fire. Firelight stained the growing darkness and wood smoke stung Lassiter's nostrils. Every eye was on the two big men facing each other in the waning light.

Sanlee spoke in a rush of words for Lassiter's ears only. "I like the way you stand up to a man, Lassiter.

Once Millie marries Rep, I'll hire you on to ramrod the two outfits. . . ."

"I'll be moving along by then. I'm a drifter at heart. . . ."

But Sanlee shook his head stubbornly. "I got me a woman I figure to marry. An' she wants to go out to Frisco for a spell. An' I aim to oblige. But I need a tough man to leave behind while I show Isobel some of the world she's got an itch to see. Don't make up your mind now, Lassiter, but keep it under your hat. We'll talk later."

Abruptly, Sanlee stalked over to the cook fire, where he picked up a steaming coffeepot from the coals. As Lassiter rode out, he was filling a tin cup.

From the edge of camp, Lassiter glanced over his shoulder at Millie's tent, which could barely be seen now in the darkness. It was close enough to where Sanlee had been sitting for her to have overheard every word. Not only had she been thwarted when she apparently had run off with Vince Tevis, but now her brother was going to use her as a bargaining chip to merge Chandler's Box C with Diamond Eight.

Pity for her plight deepened in him. He was remembering the excitement in Rep Chandler's voice when talking about marrying again. At the time Lassiter had had no idea the middle-aged rancher had his eye on a girl Millie Sanlee's age.

After roundup he'd warn Chandler of Sanlee's intentions toward Box C. Chandler might believe him. On the other hand, his reaction might be the same as it had been when Lassiter mentioned the three names Sanlee had written out.

"Brad was just joshin'," Chandler had said.

Well, Lassiter would finish roundup and drive the

Box C herd to railhead where they would be sold, as per his agreement with Chandler. Then he would do what he could for Millie.

Meanwhile, he'd let Sanlee sweat. On the day he told Chandler he was quitting, he would corner Sanlee and settle up for the death of Vince Tevis.

Then he would be off to new horizons, providing he had his usual gunfighter's luck against Sanlee. Of course, he was under no illusions, knowing that quite possibly one day he would meet a better man.

But he hoped when the gun smoke cleared, Sanlee would be dead. Millie would probably inherit Diamond Eight. At least she'd have that much.

With that settled in his mind, he ate supper and rolled up in his blankets. Sleep didn't come easily and it seemed only an hour had passed before Herrera was shaking him awake to take a turn as nighthawk with the herd.

Two days later, Ad Deverax was back in the Santos country, after a lengthy detour all the way down from Ardon, New Mexico. . . .

7

That morning Brad Sanlee was called aside by Doug Krinkle. Sanlee had just missed a cast with his rope and was in an ugly mood. His broad, bearded face bore numerous scratches from tangling with a steer in a thicket.

"Deverax is back," Krinkle said, cupping his hands to shout above the noise of yelling men and pounding cattle.

"Bolin with him?" Sanlee demanded.

"Ad's alone," Krinkle replied, his heavily freckled face tight with concern.

"If the son of a bitch wants his job back, tell him to try the moon."

"Ad's got somethin' to tell you. It's important, he claims."

"Where the hell's he been all this time? Likely layin' up in some *congal* with a chica."

"He's been in a hospital up at Wheeler City."

"Hospital?"

"He's shot bad, Brad." Krinkle gestured at a wagon.

Sanlee scowled, wound his catch rope, then mounted up and rode over to where Deverax was lying in the bed of a ranch wagon.

"What the hell happened to you?" Sanlee asked the tall man who lay on straw in the wagon. Deverax was so thinned down that Sanlee hardly recognized him. Through the dirty, unbuttoned shirt could be seen a pack of stained bandages.

"I know the fella's here," Deverax gasped. "The one that done it. I seen him here. . . ."

"Done what, for Chris' sakes?"

"Killed Bolin an' put a bullet in me. Leastwise I think Bolin's dead. I rode like hell. He was trailin' me but it rained one night an' I gave him the slip. But I was so bad by then, I had to hunt up a doc. . . ."

"Who the hell you talkin' about, anyhow?"

Krinkle cut in. "He saw Lassiter a while ago. He says it's him."

Sanlee drew a deep breath. *"Lassiter?"*

Deverax nodded weakly. "Doug says it's his name."

Sanlee jerked his thumb at Krinkle. "Get back to work, Doug." He didn't want too many details of the New Mexico venture spread about. Deverax and Bolin had been his two most trusted underlings, which was why he had taken them along on the hunt for the runaway Millie.

When Krinkle was gone, Sanlee leaned into the wagon. "Tell me about it, Ad."

Deverax was so weak he could speak only a few words at a time. "You told me an' . . . Bolin . . . to stay behind . . . an' at full dark to finish off Tevis. . . .

This Lassiter was there by then . . . in the house. . . . I thought Bolin got him sure, but the next thing I knew, Bolin is down an' I'm hit bad. . . ."

"Lassiter," Sanlee said softly through his teeth. "Then it wasn't a coincidence, his coming to Texas." Sanlee could speak decent English when he felt like it. "How'd Lassiter find out about me?"

"Tevis, I reckon. Your bullet didn't finish him, remember?"

"You get back to the ranch an' keep your mouth shut, Ad. You hear me?"

Deverax nodded. Then Sanlee shouted at the older ranch hand who had driven Deverax out to the roundup camp. "You get him home, pronto."

Sanlee stood in the hot spring sunlight, sweating. He thought about Lassiter and all that had happened. Then, with a fierce grin, he mounted up and returned to the roundup.

The next stretch of brush country to be worked for cattle was the most dangerous. A rider had to be constantly alert to the many hazards that could end his life in the flick of an eyelash.

Herrera and most of the vaqueros were mounted on small Spanish ponies. That day they rode into the black brush with its thorns like spiked fingers ready to tear cloth or the flesh of rider or horse. Whenever the vaqueros were riding down an evasive bull or a raging cow with her calf their shouts of "Ai-i-i-i!" rang through the heavy undergrowth. Recklessly they rode with ropes tied fast to the saddle horns. The big Chihuahua steers were nimble and smart, with horns that could rip like a saber into the tough hide of horses or impale a man.

Their first casualty was Tony Jerez.

It had been a grueling day in the hot and sticky hell of the Texas jungle. Lassiter had just coiled his rope for a return to the fray. He had helped bring in a half-dozen mavericks and waited until the brands were parceled out, one for each ranch. When he started riding after a big cow with her calf he heard a bellowing to his right and a great crashing in the brush. He reined in and saw a red-eyed ladino bulling his way through the thicket like a loaded, runaway freight wagon. A noose was anchored over the great spread of horns. Behind the roaring beast pounded Tony Jerez, trying to keep up because the other end of the rope was tied to his saddle horn. Jerez lost his sombrero to the brush and his long hair streamed like a black mane in the wind.

"Use your knife!" Lassiter shouted to him. "Cut the bastard loose!"

But Jerez either didn't hear him above the wild crashing in the brush or was determined to prove his manhood and not accept defeat by a bull, no matter how big or ferocious. He dug in his Chihuahua spurs and the wild-eyed pony leaped ahead. Its coat was damp with sweat and in places the winter hair had been scraped off by the lethal brush. Again Lassiter yelled advice, which Jerez chose to ignore. His white teeth gleamed in his dark face, reminding Lassiter of miniature tombstones. A chill ran down his spine at the thought.

Swearing under his breath, Lassiter drew his rifle and tried to pump a bullet into the skull of the maddened ladino. But at the last moment the big animal swerved, and it and the pursuing vaquero disappeared into the stifling ocean of brush.

As Lassiter pounded after them, he saw that Jerez was maneuvering the ladino toward the holding ground. He saw the vaquero pull hard on his reins in an attempt to slow the crazed animal. The Spanish pony dug in its heels but there was no halting the steer. It was shaking its head, trying to rid itself of the noose that had trapped its horns. It pounded across the clearing. Branders yelled warnings and leaped back from their fires.

The ladino trampled one of the fires, scattering embers. Other riders reined in to stare at what could be a potential tragedy. Jerez could have freed himself of his mistake by shooting the savage bull. And mistake it had been—a rope aimed for a hind leg had instead settled over the horns. Jerez had missed his cast and now seemed determined to bring his quarry to bay.

But as the pony settled its weight, the rope stretched taut as a banjo string, the ladino suddenly changed directions. With foam dripping from its nostrils and jaws, it charged directly at the pony. One horn tip splintered the breastbone. The Chihuahua steer quickly withdrew from the floundering horse and turned on its rider, who had flung himself to the ground, landing lightly on his feet. Now Jerez was waving his arms, trying to confuse the beast and get it tangled up in the brush by the rope stretched from steer horns to the saddle of the downed pony.

Again Lassiter fired. His bullet nicked a horn. By then the steer had lunged at Jerez and Lassiter had to spin his horse to get out of the way. When he looked back over his shoulder he saw to his horror that Jerez was running, and that there was still plenty of slack in the rope now between the charging beast and the dying horse. It caught Jerez at the edge of the clearing. With a great upsweep of its horn, Jerez was lifted off the ground and hurled headfirst into the thick trunk of a mesquite. Even above the pounding hooves was the terrible sound of a neck bone snapping.

Before the steer could turn and trample the body of its enemy, Lassiter was finally able to place a bullet between its maddened eyes. The big steer took a couple of wobbly steps, then crashed to earth.

Lassiter was just dismounting when a bullet whipped past his ear, followed by the sharp crack of a rifle. He spun in time to see Doug Krinkle lowering his weapon.

"I figured to put a bullet in that big Chihuahua," the freckled Diamond Eight rider called. "But I see you got him."

Krinkle rode away.

Lassiter was hot with rage.

"One of these days, Sanlee," Lassiter said softly in his anger.

With the aroma of yellow huisache blossoms lacing the air, they buried Jerez. There he would lie for all eternity in an unmarked grave.

That evening the Box C crew ate supper in silence, each man wondering—not fearfully but realistically—if tomorrow he might be the next one buried. They had a code of living hard and, if it came time, to die hard. It was agreed among them that it was better for a man to lose his life than his pride. Jerez had attempted to erase a mistake by heroically challenging the great steer. He had lost the gamble. It was as simple as that.

Sanlee came tramping up, wiping his large bearded face with a bandanna. "That crazy Mex," he said to Lassiter. "More bone in his head than sense. It's why I never hire one of the bastards."

Lassiter often wondered what would have happened had not Sanlee turned abruptly on his heel and walked away. It was much later before Lassiter could calm down after the insult to the dead rider.

Several times during the night, Lassiter thought about Sanlee's proposition to make him ramrod of Diamond Eight and Box C. Each time it crossed his mind, he smiled coldly. His working for Brad Sanlee would be the longest day in Texas history. He'd bide his time before calling Sanlee for the murder of Vince Tevis. His old friend was no doubt a misguided Lothario who had been carried away by Millie Sanlee's fetching figure and those intense black eyes.

Two days later Rep Chandler appeared at roundup camp in a hack wagon. With his splinted leg, it was awkward for him to get out of the small wagon.

Lassiter had just ridden in with a dozen steers that he and his men had rousted from a tornillo thicket. Lassiter rode over and dismounted. Chandler offered his hand, which Lassiter shook. Then the rancher, using a cane, limped over to a large flat rock next to a fernlike growth of juajuillo and sat down. He removed his hat. Perspiration dampened his sparse brown hair. "I told Brad Sanlee I never had a foreman as good as you," Chandler said.

Lassiter laughed. "What'd he say to that?"

"He said if that's what I wanted, that's the way it'd be."

Lassiter shook his head.

"You seem skeptical," Chandler said with a frown.

"I am."

"Sanlee will leave you alone—believe me on that. . . ."

"I'm not afraid of him."

"That's what I like about you, Lassiter—your toughness. He'll leave you alone because I'll be marryin' his sister."

"She's agreeable, I suppose," Lassiter said, watching the rancher's face.

Chandler rubbed his jaw. "I don't rightly know, to tell the truth. But it makes no mind whether she is or not."

Lassiter couldn't forget Millie's frightened face. "She oughta have a say about who she marries."

"I reckon you don't know how things are done down here."

"One thing I do know is right from wrong!"

But Chandler was talking about his first wife and not even listening to Lassiter. "When me an' my first wife was married, she didn't like me worth a damn. She was fourteen an' I was four years older. But my pa said marry her. Her pa said the same to her. It worked out purty good, considerin'. Twenty-eight years later she up an' got a sickness an' died on me. So it'll be the same with me an' Millie."

"Things have changed since you got married the first time."

"I aim to take Millie over to Austin, then go up to New York to see them tall buildings they got there. Hell, I'm over hatin' the blue bellies. The war's long over." He leaned over to give Lassiter a friendly slap on the arm. "I'm countin' on you to run things while I'm gone."

"You and Sanlee."

"What'd you mean by that?"

"Nothing. The hell with it. But as soon as roundup's over and the cows sold, I'll be gettin' an itch to see what's on the yonder side of the mountain."

"Ain't no mountain around here."

Lassiter gave him a hard smile. "Just a way of putting things. But I stay in a place just so long, then I've got to push on."

"You can't quit on me. Hell, I . . ."

"You've got a good man in Luis Herrera."

Chandler fidgeted on the flat rock. Men were drifting in and out of camp. Some helped themselves to coffee from the big pot on the coals of the cook fire. Others swapped a jaded horse for a fresh one.

"I already let Luis get up the ladder farther than I should, likely," Chandler said.

"He's segundo. Let him go up a step. Why not, for Chris' sakes?"

"It just ain't done—not around here it ain't, anyhow."

Lassiter guessed the problem. Chandler stubbornly refused to advance a good man like Herrera because it was the local custom to have only Anglos in positions of authority. Memories of the Alamo, it seemed, still clouded some Texas minds. One thing Lassiter couldn't abide was injustice, whether to a girl like Millie Sanlee or a man like Luis Herrera.

"You got any idea why Sanlee is trying to force his sister to marry you?" he demanded, anger spilling over.

"Now see here . . ."

It was as far as Chandler got because Lassiter unloaded, telling him of Sanlee's plans. "To move in on you and eventually take over," he finished.

"Just how the hell do you know that, Lassiter?"

"He told me."

Chandler studied him a moment, then began to laugh. "Brad was just joshin' you. I watched that boy grow up. Me an' his daddy was friends. . . ."

"My strong hunch is that Sanlee meant every word."

"What if he did?" Chandler jerked at an end of his mustache. "With you as my ramrod, he won't make a move against me." Chandler grunted and got to his feet. "I'm meetin' with Millie in town tomorrow at noon at the Hartney Store. I better get home an' rest up my leg." He gave a weak grin and limped with his cane to the hack wagon.

Yesterday, Millie had been allowed to go home, Lassiter had learned from others, and put in the charge of a dour housekeeper named Elva Dowd. He wanted to see her and thought about tomorrow at noon in Santos. Just thinking of seeing her again pumped excitement through his veins. . . .

8

"You had your chance an' you wasted a shot into mesquite instead of Lassiter's hard head." Sanlee was standing next to Doug Krinkle at one end of O'Leary's bar. He had ordered Krinkle to go along when he escorted Millie back to the home place. Elva Dowd, big-armed and toothy, would keep a subdued Millie in hand.

"I'll have another chance at Lassiter," Krinkle said and gave a hitch at his gun belt.

"That son of a bitch is just plain lucky. Deverax an' Bolin shootin' at him in a two-by-four shack an' by God, both of 'em missin' the bastard. Then Lassiter puts a bullet in Deverax an' kills Bolin."

"Luck's like sand in an hourglass. It runs just so long."

"Somebody told you that. You never thought it up by yourself."

"I read it somewhere," Krinkle admitted. It rankled that he'd had Lassiter right in his rifle sight. And in all the confusion of the vaquero getting killed and the yelling, he could have gotten away with it. But at the last minute Lassiter had turned his head. Talk about luck. Then Lassiter had given him a cold stare that chilled his backbone.

"I'll have to get Lassiter before he gets me," Krinkle said after a minute. He swished some whiskey around in his glass, then drained it. "He knows damn well I was tryin' for him at roundup."

"Well, for Chris' sakes, next time make sure of him."

"Maybe you oughta make a try for him yourself, Brad," Krinkle suggested slyly, but he was ready to duck in case Sanlee swung his hand at him, which he was known to do when his temper exploded. But today Sanlee accepted it with a tight grin.

"If it comes to the point where fellas I pay to do a job can't get it done, then I'll face up to the bastard. It'll be the end of the legend of Lassiter. I'll blow him outta his boots."

"You can do it, Brad."

"I'm damn sure of that. But meanwhile . . ." Sanlee gave Krinkle a hard look.

"Yeah, yeah, I'll figure somethin' out."

"*Do* it!" Sanlee snapped. "I pay good money for you an' Doane to run risks, which you two didn't earn the day you tried to corral him on the east road."

Memory of the suddenness of Lassiter's attack that day caused Krinkle's freckled face to redden. And to have had Isobel Hartney witness the humiliation was almost too much.

"Hey, Doug, you ol' son of a bitch you!"

Krinkle swung around at the sound of a familiar voice. "Cuz!" he cried, laughing, and he and the tall, scar-faced man gave each other the *abrazo*. It was

Krinkle's cousin, Sam Busher. Krinkle broke out of the embrace of his kin and introduced him to Sanlee, who acknowledged it with a jerk of his head. He was eyeing Busher's gun in a cut-down holster. Then he studied the scars on his round face. There were four scars, two of them deep.

"Some gal use a knife when you had your britches off?" Sanlee asked thinly, referring to the scars.

"Nope," Busher said. "I had a fair-sized poke on me. Four hombres held me while a fifth used his blade."

"Did they get your poke?"

"Yeah. But later I got them and the money they was carryin'."

"All five of 'em?" Sanlee was interested and put his back to the bar, elbows hooked over the lip.

"All five," Busher admitted modestly. "An' what they had on 'em was a sight more'n they took off me."

"Did the law ever get after you for it?"

"Not for that. A few other things, though." Busher's smile was hard. His clothing was worn and dusty as if he'd traveled hard and far. Sanlee matched his grin, then nudged Krinkle.

"I figure you an' your cuz just might handle Lassiter."

"Point him out," Busher said. "I'll handle him alone."

Sanlee shook his head. "When it happens, I want Krinkle to face up to him. An' I want you at Lassiter's back. He's fast an' I don't want any slip-ups. I saw him work once an' I know."

"I rode down this way figurin' maybe Doug could point me to a job. Looks like I got one. How's the pay?"

"Ask your cuz."

Busher turned inquiringly to Krinkle, who said, "Pay's good."

"Damned good," Sanlee added, "if you're successful, that is." He let it hang there while Busher thought it over, then nodded. Sanlee called to O'Leary for a clean glass, then poured whiskey from his bottle for the three of them.

"I want you an' Doug to stick with me wherever I go," Sanlee said quietly when O'Leary had departed. "Not right with me, you understand, but close enough. So I can give you a signal in a big hurry."

"You want this Lassiter real bad," Busher said with a smile.

"On a dark night I want to be able to stomp on his grave an' bellow at the moon."

Busher and Krinkle laughed.

Then Busher looked Sanlee in the eye. "How much pay, in dollars, not talk?"

"One thousand each."

"The sooner you give us that signal, the sooner I can start spendin' the money," Busher said, a pleased look on his scarred face.

Sanlee nodded, feeling confident that Lassiter was as good as dead.

The following day, Lassiter glanced at the sky. It was mid-morning, and he could make Santos well before noon. He had a hunch that Millie would be early for her meeting with Chandler. He told Herrera to take over for him and rode in the direction of town.

With most able-bodied men hired on extra for roundup, the town was practically deserted. Spring heat bore down and some old men were in chairs under an overhang out of the sun. Women in tight-waisted dresses fanned themselves as they picked up supplies or examined the latest in yard goods at the Hartney Store.

Isobel Hartney saw Lassiter coming with a long-legged stride, his dark face a blend of the piratical and benevolent. She quickly removed an apron, smoothed her yellow hair and put on a bright smile.

"Mr. Lassiter! It's an honor to have you in my store. What can I show you?"

He remembered her from that day on the east road. He stood by one of the crowded counters, admiring her. Women customers looked at Lassiter, then at Isobel Hartney standing tall in a blue silk dress, much too fancy for a small-town Texas store. Some of them exchanged glances and spoke together in whispers behind fingertips.

Isobel knew they were gossiping about her and she didn't give a hoot and a holler what they said or thought. She found Lassiter to be an interesting man and was toying with the idea that he just might be a companion—until she tired of him—which she did with all the others. One day she'd probably get around to marrying Brad Sanlee, but until that day. . . .

He stood at a counter, his dark face tight, looking over the customers in the store. Isobel waved away one of her clerks and personally sold Lassiter a sack of tobacco and some papers. He had just paid her and she was about to initiate some bright conversation when he stiffened at the sight of someone through a front window.

Isobel stood on her tiptoes so she could see who he was staring at. Her smooth forehead creased in a faint frown as she saw Millie Sanlee just dismounting at the tie rack in the big vacant lot beside the store. Millie had her black hair peeled back with the usual sullen look on her face. Her brother Brad was with her.

He said something and crossed the street to the saloon.

Lassiter had gone outside and removed his hat as he stood talking to Millie. "Damn," said Isobel under her breath.

In the vacant lot, Lassiter was saying, "I heard you were coming to town. So I gambled that I'd have a chance to talk to you."

"You're Lassiter. My brother told me about you."

"I'm here to give you a hand, if you'll take it."

She glanced across the street and up the block at the long two-story building that housed O'Leary's. Sunlight was reflected off the windows. She saw her brother go inside.

"It's about you marrying Rep Chandler," Lassiter said when she continued to stare at the saloon. "Millie, are you listening?"

She faced him, a faint smile on her lips. "Let's take a walk," she suggested and started for another vacant lot behind the store. It was deeply rutted from wagon wheels.

"My real name is Millicent," she said with a little laugh. "My mother named me. I love it. But nobody ever calls me that."

"I will . . . Millicent."

"You don't have to." Smiling wistfully, she looked up into his face as they walked together. Then she sobered. "My brother's in town."

"I saw him."

"You're not afraid?"

"Come what may."

Her eyes were excited for a moment, then the fire went out of them. "You mentioned Rep Chandler."

"Yeah, it's what I want to talk to you about."

"I've concluded that the only door left open for me is to marry him."

"You're your own boss. You can do what you want. You ran away once, why not again? I'll help. . . ."

"Brad would hunt me down like he did last time."

"No . . ."

"Brad says Vince was your friend. Rep told him."

"A good friend," Lassiter said, the scene of death coldly etched in his mind.

"All the time we were together, Vince Tevis never made a move on me."

"What if he did? I sure wouldn't hold it against you. All I want to do is help. . . ."

"On nights if we had a roof over our heads, Vince gave me the bed. He slept on the floor in his bedroll."

"Millicent, Millicent, I don't *care*."

"Before that, we slept out till one night horse thieves hit us. From then on, we went by stage-coach." Her voice caught. "So Vince died. I'm sorry."

"Your brother killed him. . . ."

"No. It was Bolin who shot Vince. I'm pretty sure of it."

"I don't believe that."

"But it's true." She described Bolin so accurately that Lassiter knew he was the one killed in front of the adobe shack. But he still didn't believe her story. It seemed she was trying to protect Sanlee. But why, after the way he had treated her?

"I knew that if I ran this time, Brad would hunt me down if it took five years. You see, he's made his plans and no one better interfere. So that's why I've decided to marry Mr. Chandler. It's what Brad wants. And it'll save trouble in the end."

"He's threatened you in some way."

"My mind's made up." Her black hair had the sheen of pure silk in the sunlight.

"It's your life, but I think you're foolish." They had halted next to a storage shed beside the store. Across the vacant lot on the west side of the store was a saddle shop, next to that was the bank.

"If you stay on as Chandler's foreman, my brother will be afraid to make his move."

"Did Chandler suggest that?"

Instead of answering, Millie's black eyes sparkled. "Oh, I know what Brad wants to do. He thinks I'm weak. He's always planned to use me as a pawn." The corners of her generous mouth were firm. "He thinks I'm worthless. A lot of people do. . . ."

"That's fool talk, Millicent."

She gave a little laugh. "Oh, for heaven's sake, call me Millie. I'm more than used to it by now."

Lassiter tried to argue against the marriage, but she was adamant. "Brad Sanlee is my half brother. His father and my mother were . . . friends. Even before the wife, Brad's mother, died. I'm only telling you this because everyone in this part of the country knows it and you'll hear it soon enough." She sounded bitter.

"What happened after the old man's wife died? Did he marry your mother?"

"Things went on just as before. My father lived at the ranch, my mother and I here in Santos."

"He never married your mother, then."

Millie gave a small laugh. "My mother was half Mexican. And the old man had lost three uncles in the fighting when General Santa Anna was driven out of Texas. Some memories are the longest."

"I know," Lassiter said, thinking of Luis Herrera.

"But after my mother died, I guess Mr. Sanlee's conscience got to bothering him. Until then, I didn't know he had one. Anyway, he brought me into his house to raise as his daughter—despite my so-called mixed blood." They were walking back when she suddenly halted and gripped his arm. "Stay on as foreman, won't you?"

"I don't know about that. . . ."

"At least for a year."

"And what about you?" he asked her. "What about your life?"

"I'll be a good wife to Mr. Chandler. I'll hold up my end of the bargain. But I'll need help against my brother. Will you do it, Lassiter?" She gave him a sad smile, stood abruptly on her toes and pressed warm lips against his cheek.

Then she started walking away, the fringe of the leather riding skirt whipping around booted ankles. There was a sadness to her beauty that touched him deeply. He liked her and felt sorry for her. But did he owe her a year out of his life? She had rejected his offer to help her run away and elected instead to submit to her half-brother's wishes, and marry the man he had selected. But still she had asked for Lassiter's protection. Maybe he'd stay until she was married and settled. Then it was up to Chandler to protect not only his wife but the ranch.

Then the reason for him coming to Texas in the first place came crowding back. And he was remembering what she had told him about Vince Tevis's death.

He found her in front of the store, peering nervously down the twisting road in the direction that Rep Chandler would take from his Box C.

He saw her look around at him. "Brad can see us from O'Leary's. You shouldn't be seen with me."

"No matter what you said, I think he killed Vince Tevis."

"No."

"You're trying to save your brother's life," he said coldly, "by claiming that Bolin . . ."

"You killed Bolin. So you said. So you already avenged poor Vince."

"You'd stick up for Sanlee? After all he's done to you and the way he humiliated you at roundup? Then forcing you into marrying a man twice your age or more?"

"After all, we did have the same father, Brad and I. . . ."

Lassiter gave a harsh laugh and shook his head. He started to speak, but she stepped close, her lovely face showing sudden strain.

"I hoped you'd leave," she said in a tight whisper, "so I kept talking. . . . Now I've got to tell you. Doug Krinkle is . . ."

She broke off, a look of terror in her eyes.

"Krinkle is . . . *what?*" he demanded, looking both ways along the nearly deserted street.

"While we were talking, I saw him slip out the back door of the saddle shop next door."

Lassiter wheeled, one hand clamped to his gun. He stared at the adjoining building beyond the weed-grown lot. It was one story of weathered lumber with a parapet along the roof. A sign on the side in black letters said: SIMON'S SADDLE SHOP.

And at that moment there was a rattle of wagon wheels, the hoofbeats of a hard-running team. Lassiter jerked his head around and saw Rep Chandler driving up in his hack wagon, a broad smile under his mustache as he saw Millie. Then it faded into a look of surprise as he spotted Lassiter standing beside her.

From a corner of his eye, Lassiter finally spotted movement, possibly Krinkle. It came from the storage shed behind the store. He gave Millie a hard shove that sent her stumbling toward the front door of the store. And at the same time he yelled at Chandler. "Get out, Rep! I smell a trap!"

Chandler, with his splinted leg resting on the dashboard, awkwardly hauled in the spirited team. And as he brought them to a halt, there was a gunshot. It came from the roof of the saddle shop. A bullet splintered a corner of the wagon seat.

Lassiter had already noticed movement on the roof. He saw part of a face and the gleam of a rifle barrel over the edge of the wooden parapet. And as if jerked by wires from an observation balloon, a man popped into view on the roof. As women began screaming, he dropped the rifle. He lurched to the parapet, blood pumping from a hole in his neck. He bowed low as if to inspect the descent of his falling weapon. Then he pitched over and followed it to the ground. Lassiter had a glimpse of a badly scarred face.

9

"I'm callin' you, Lassiter!" It was the screech of Doug Krinkle in an off-key voice. He had been running from the protection of the shed along the west side of the store. Now he had halted, his mouth hanging open, probably because the man on the roof had fired too soon and taken him by surprise. Now Krinkle was snapping into action and apparently going ahead with the plan, whatever it was. But his gun was already out and you don't call a man unless your weapon is holstered. Obviously, he had been told to shout the challenge and so he had done so, belatedly.

He was coming at a run, firing at a corner of the store where Lassiter had ducked. Millie was crouched near the door. Women inside were still hysterical. Rep Chandler had backed his team and was reaching on the floorboards for a rifle. Adobe chips were flying as bullets dug into the wall of the store, which were fired erratically by a nervous Krinkle. The man was running hard now; Lassiter could hear his footsteps. And in another handful of seconds, Millie and Rep Chandler could be in danger.

Krinkle's third shot was aimed chest high as he swung away from the store for a glimpse of his target. But the bullet went screaming in ricochet off the wall. At that moment Lassiter sprang into a crouching run into the open before Krinkle could fire again. He glimpsed the look of surprise on Krinkle's face and saw the man recover quickly to try and bring down Lassiter's sprinting figure with a snap shot. But it missed. As Krinkle thumbed back the hammer for another desperate try, Lassiter shot him twice—once high in the chest, the second just above the belt buckle.

As Krinkle collapsed, someone yelled a warning. Lassiter spun around in time to see Brad Sanlee just kicking through the weeds of the vacant lot. He held a big .45. In his wild run, Sanlee's hat sailed off and his coarse, reddish hair bounced at each step.

The .45 came up, but not aimed at Lassiter. Sanlee fired into the weeds. "He was tryin' for your back, Lassiter!" Sanlee shouted. "I got him for you!"

Men were coming at a run, some of them crowding around the one who had fallen from the roof. Sanlee had just fired into the side of the skull.

A white-faced Millie came to grip Lassiter by his arm. "Are you all right?" she breathed.

He nodded and saw a stricken Rep Chandler at a limping run toward Millie. Lassiter gave her a shove toward the rancher and turned to look at Krinkle. He pushed through a circle of men to stare down at the crumpled figure.

"Dead as last night's beer," a man said with a shaky laugh. "That was some shootin', mister," he added to Lassiter.

Lassiter smeared a shirt sleeve across his forehead and watched Sanlee lumber up.

"That was close," Sanlee said, breathing hard from the run. "I saw him about to make a try for your back."

The man was already dead. I'll bet on it!

Lassiter kept his thoughts to himself. Swiftly, he punched out empties from his smoking .44. They bounced along the hard ground, then he reloaded.

A round man with a jiggling belly under an immaculate white shirt came hurrying up to stand next to Sanlee. "I'm Arthur Hobart of the bank," he said to Lassiter. "You certainly owe Mr. Sanlee a vote of thanks. He saved your bacon."

Lassiter wondered about that. The bank was beyond the saddle shop. But, of course, Hobart might have been in the street when the shootout took place. He saw Hobart turn away, give Sanlee a small smile, a pat on the arm, then walk away through the crowd. In Lassiter's mind, a strong affiliation had been established between Diamond Eight and the Bank of Santos.

Sanlee was helping his sister into Chandler's wagon, where she sat, stiff as a mud wall, pale about the mouth.

"I reckon Krinkle carried a grudge on account of you messin' him up the other day," Sanlee said over his shoulder to Lassiter. "The other fella was his no-account cousin. I reckon Krinkle talked him into backin' his hand."

"I reckon," Lassiter said dryly, his eyes as cold as a sleet-driven sky.

"You could use a drink, Lassiter," Sanlee suggested. "Rep's got some talkin' to do to my sister. Let's you an' me go over to O'Leary's an' . . ."

"I'm due back at roundup."

"Suit yourself," Sanlee said shortly. He walked over to where a ring of men were staring down at Krinkle. "Damn it, Doug," he said to the corpse. "You an' your temper. I told you that holdin' a grudge can get a man killed. An' it sure did."

Lassiter walked stiffly to where he had left his horse. Millie was rattling away in Chandler's wagon, and Sanlee was crossing to the saloon.

As Lassiter untied the reins at the rear of the store, Isobel Hartney opened the back door and leaned out, blond and beautiful. She was wearing her apron again and a stub of yellow pencil was behind an ear.

"The other day you were lucky, Lassiter. Today you had even more luck. That's twice. I dread to think of a third time."

"Tell you the truth, I'm not lookin' forward to it."

He gave her a tight smile and rode out.

Only after a mile or so from town did he begin to let down. He could have used the whiskey Sanlee had suggested. But Lassiter had no intention of drinking with him. He knew as sure as there was sun in the Texas sky that Sanlee had put the pair up to it. Kill both of them, Chandler and Lassiter. Then Sanlee could bargain away his half-sister in another direction, perhaps with one of the ranchers whose names had appeared on the death list.

Strangely enough, the cattle drive to railhead went without incident. With two money sacks holding $74,000 in cash, Lassiter made a much faster return trip. While away, he had done a lot of thinking and concluded that his obligation to Rep Chandler had been fulfilled. It was time to settle the business he still felt he had with Sanlee, despite Millie's insistence that her brother was not involved in the death of Vince Tevis. With the Sanlee matter out of the way at last, he would head for Arizona. He liked the country and had friends there.

Upon his arrival back at Box C, he was surprised to find the ranch yard strung with Chinese lanterns. There was a bustle of activity, men moving long tables into the yard. The Romero brothers, who did all the barbecuing for the area, were digging their pits.

Rep Chandler spotted him through a window and came limping to the door with a cane. He grinned broadly. His leg was no longer splinted. "Thank the good Lord you got home in time, Lassiter. Millie will be awful pleased. . . ."

"Time for what?" Lassiter asked as he handed over the money sacks. Chandler hardly gave them a glance.

"Why, for the weddin', that's what. Only time we could get the reverend, as he's due north in a coupla days."

"Listen, Rep . . ."

"Millie wants you to be best man." Chandler clapped him on the back. "An' I want it, too. It'll make that little gal awful happy, I can tell you."

"Being best man is Sanlee's job. What's he say about it?"

"She had it out with him. He backed down."

Lassiter wondered about that. Well, would it hurt him to stay for the wedding? Lassiter asked himself.

It turned out to be one of the biggest events for that part of Texas since the war. Neighbors that Chandler hadn't seen in two years or more, because of vast distances, were in attendance. The Romero boys had lined their barbecue pits with rocks. Fires had been built and allowed to burn down to coals. Then great chunks of beef were put into the pits, covered with rocks, then gunny sacks and allowed to roast.

Early on the day of the wedding the aroma of cooking food permeated the spring air. The cleared area beyond the nearest barn was filled with wagons and teams. Nearby, tents were being pitched to accommodate those guests not lucky enough to get one of the spare bedrooms in the big adobe ranch house.

Some of Herrera's friends had been hired to supply the music. With guitar, fiddles and cornets, it was lively. Most of the guests, Lassiter noticed, mingled freely with the Mexicans. Only a few were still stiff-necked with their undiminished memories of Mexican rule in Texas.

Sanlee arrived with a great fanfare, a dozen of his Diamond Eight riders on horses decorated with bunting. In the wagon, which Sanlee was driving with a broad smile on his bearded face, was Millie. She smiled demurely. Their wagon was colorfully bedecked with cornflowers.

They rolled into the yard accompanied by a great shout from the many guests. The gaunt preacher in sober black was behind them in another rig. Because it was bad luck for the bridegroom to see his intended before the wedding, Millie was hustled into the house through a side door by some of the excited ladies.

Lassiter, wearing a black suit, came face to face with Sanlee, who greeted him enthusiastically. A beaming Sanlee thrust out his big hand.

With so many looking on, Lassiter reluctantly shook hands with him. Smiling faintly, Lassiter studied the gray eyes, wondering just what really went on in that crafty Sanlee brain.

Men hustled Sanlee away for a drink where other male guests were crowded around a long table holding bins of bottled beer, cooled by well water. There were jugs of whiskey and bottles of wine from San Antone. Children ran whooping through the crowd until it came time for the ceremony. Then they were shushed into silence.

Rep Chandler, in a dark suit and white shirt, was determined not to use his cane during the ceremony. He had taken a lot of joshing from the men on the subject of his bad leg curtailing activities on the wedding night.

Millie's face was pale but beautiful. However, her dark eyes seemed sad to Lassiter. He felt sorry for her, sorry she hadn't been bold enough to take the gamble and get away from her half-brother once and for all. But apparently she lacked the courage and now it would soon be too late. She and her new husband would be Brad Sanlee's neighbors, for better or for worse. Lassiter hoped for her sake it wasn't the latter.

He stepped from the house with her. Not a word was spoken as they walked along an aisle formed by the beaming guests. Some of the women, however, were already red-eyed, a preamble to frontier tears shed equally between funerals and weddings.

The Reverend Grant, with a thin face slick with perspiration and a wilted collar, kept glancing at a large gold watch. He had a stage to catch, and this thankfully kept the ceremony brief.

When it was over and everyone was swarming up to offer congratulations and men to kiss the bride, Lassiter backed away, deciding to forego that pleasure. He had taken only a few steps when her soft voice arrested him.

"Lassiter," she called with false gaiety. "Isn't my husband's foreman going to do me honor?" She held out her hands to him when the crowd parted to let her through.

"Of course," Lassiter said with a stiff smile.

He met her warm lips with his own. Her dark eyes glowed. As he felt the pressure of her softness against him, he experienced a swift reaction. Careful, Lassiter, he warned himself. Don't start building foolish dreams in your head. She's another man's wife. . . .

10

As Millie moved down the line of waiting and eager males, Lassiter saw Isobel Hartney watching him. She was wearing a dress of green silk that brought out the fire in her eyes. Her lovely face was lighted with a smile as she walked over.

"I haven't seen you since that terrible day in town," she said, coming close, her clothing making a soft rustle. "Two dead men." She shivered and hunched her splendid shoulders. "How fortunate that Brad saw that other man about to put a bullet in your back."

Lassiter nodded, not trusting himself to speak.

"I have a feeling you think perhaps Brad prompted that horrible business. But I assure you he didn't. I saw the whole thing through a window."

"I didn't realize Sanlee had a witness," he said evenly.

"You're a very interesting man, Lassiter. Brad has mentioned you several times."

"I'm not surprised," he said with a hard smile. He

was remembering that Sanlee had told him about wedding plans for an Isobel. This one, of course.

"Contrary to what you might think, Brad likes you."

It crossed Lassiter's mind that Sanlee had put her up to paying him a compliment. But why? he wondered. He was jostled by exuberant wedding guests moving about the tree-shaded yard.

Isobel was studying him through pale lashes, a faint frown on her vibrant face. "Brad has planned some entertainment that he claims you might find interesting."

Something in her green eyes alerted him. "What kind of entertainment?"

But before she could reply, Sanlee came up to lay a large hand on the green sleeve of her dress. "Get yourself some whiskey, Lassiter," he bellowed half-drunkenly. He gestured at the table where men crowded like flies around a honey pot. Sanlee gave Lassiter a crooked smile, a broad wink, then moved away with Isobel Hartney, his walk unsteady. Was he really that drunk?

Lassiter couldn't help but rivet his eyes on Isobel's back as she moved through the crowd, noticing how the green dress clung, full at the shoulders, nipped in at the waist and then spreading over voluptuous hips. Halfway across the yard, she looked back at him, a little apprehensively, he thought. Then Sanlee tightened his arm in hers and hurried her away.

That day Lassiter hadn't intended to be armed. But he was alerted by what Isobel might have been about to say when interrupted by Sanlee's sudden appearance. He went to his quarters, a lean-to adjoining the main barn. There he got his .44 from a desk drawer, stuck it in his waistband, then buttoned the black coat. Everyone had agreed to Chandler's request that all guns be checked at the barn. Late arrivals were dropping off their weapons to a friend of Chandler's, who tagged each of them. They were hung on nails by the trigger guards. Nearly one whole wall was taken up with the many firearms, Lassiter noted as he passed the open doors.

Feeling more comfortable with a gun under his coat, Lassiter walked away from the barn doors. He noticed that women, mostly in summer dresses, some holding parasols, were hurrying across the yard to gather in a knot with the men. Quite a crowd was growing around someone standing on a box. Who it was Lassiter couldn't tell because a low-hanging cottonwood branch cut off the upper half of a male body. All Lassiter could see was a pair of black trousers and polished boots.

The unknown man on the box was gesturing and what he said brought a cheer from the men, exclamations of surprise and gasps from the ladies. There was much applause.

Curious, Lassiter drew closer. Above the hand-clapping and loud voices he heard his name mentioned by the speaker. He couldn't identify the voice because of all the noise.

Lassiter halted. A warning like a red-hot wire whipped through him. He saw Millie Sanlee—Chandler now—catch sight of him and squirm her way through the crowd. With the train of her wedding dress looped over one arm, her white skirts lifted, she came at a run.

"Lassiter," she gasped. "Brad's planning the most ghastly thing. . . . You've got to get out of here."

"What ghastly thing?" Even though he still could

not see the speaker, he knew now it was Sanlee. As the crowd listened now in silence, Lassiter recognized the booming voice.

". . . and don't forget to bet generously," Sanlee was shouting, "because the two combatants have promised that half of all winnings go into a fund for the widows and orphans of San Antone. . . ."

"So that's it!" Lassiter bared his teeth.

"Lassiter!" a short, bony man shouted, beckoning. "Sanlee wants you. *Step up!*"

And Sanlee brushed aside the cottonwood branch and leaned over so he could see Lassiter. At Sanlee's side towered Shorty Doane, his scarred lips smiling broadly. Doane had already removed the coat to his Sunday suit. He was rolling up a shirt sleeve on a muscular forearm.

A buxom woman in a tight-fitting brown dress wailed, "Oh, I hope there won't be blood!"

"None to speak of, Mrs. Lester," Sanlee called to her good-naturedly, which brought a bellow of laughter from the men. "Kilhaven is gonna keep time. The fight's for half an hour. At the end of that time the winner will be named—unless one of 'em ends up cold as an icy rock."

More laughter.

"Better get your coat off, Lassiter!" Sanlee called, still holding aside the cottonwood branch. His teeth gleamed through his beard.

Some of those nearby were turning to look from Lassiter to Doane, assessing each. A man voiced what was undoubtedly on the minds of many. "Sanlee, your man's a heap bigger than Chandler's. How about Chuck Hale? He's more Lassiter's size."

"Chandler's already agreed to Doane!" Sanlee shouted.

Lassiter's angry eyes searched through the crowd. "Chandler, damn him. . . ."

But Millie was clutching at Lassiter's arm, whispering, "Rep didn't know anything about it, Lassiter."

Chandler saw him at that moment. He started limping toward him, a look of concern on his flushed face. "Hell, Lassiter, don't think I had a hand in this."

But it was mostly drowned out by excited voices from the crowd anticipating a spectacle.

"I don't figure to stand up to Doane," Lassiter stated flatly, "on this day or any other!" His voice was cold. He was standing at the edge of the jabbering crowd. Slowly, he backed up until cottonwood branches poked him between the shoulder blades. When he started to step away from the trees, something hard was pressed against his back—not a tree limb this time, but something metallic.

He tensed, ready to spin around. Then it came to him that putting up a fight with a gun could endanger innocents—Millie included.

Whipped to a frenzy of excitement by Brad Sanlee's exhortations, men were crowding up to one of the tables to place their bets. Even though some of the bravest of the excited women indicated a desire to wager, they had to abstain. Other ladies who had not imbibed so freely of wines pointed out that to do so would be most unseemly. So their husbands had the full responsibility of betting money a lot of them could ill afford. But purse strings had been loosened by whiskey and the excitement during a celebration that came all too seldom to break the drabness of their daily lives. And so they were determined to enjoy the day. And wasn't it for a good cause? What more worthy than the plight of widows and orphans?

Lassiter stood with every muscle tensed as the crowd swirled away from him toward the gaming table. He knew without turning his head the nature of the object pressing so hard against his back. And he recognized the warning voice; it belonged to Joe Tige, one of Sanlee's men.

"Stand hitched," Tige hissed from the protection of cottonwoods, "or I'll bust your back with a bullet. I'm takin' your gun."

Arthur Hobart, the banker, came by. He was dry-washing his hands, grinning at Lassiter, not guessing the predicament he was in, probably not caring.

"It looks like you're in for it," he called and hurried into the crowd.

As a hand stole around Lassiter's right side and fingers groped at his belt, he again considered making a play. But Millie was directly in front of him, her back turned as she stood with fists clenched, watching the jam of men around the table. And nearby women and children were gathered as husbands and fathers piled silver and gold on the table to be placed by Kilhaven in an iron box.

Lassiter stood perfectly still and felt the .44 removed from his waistband. How did Tige know he was armed? he asked himself. Possibly, Tige had seen him rush to his quarters and suspected the reason for the haste.

Tige stepped back into the trees. Lassiter turned his head, but the burly Diamond Eight rider was gone.

Then Lassiter noticed all eyes on him. Sanlee was yelling, his gray eyes merry above the reddish beard. "Off with your coat, Lassiter!"

Millie was holding the train of her gown in a trembling hand. At her side, Rep looked around at Lassiter. For the first time, Lassiter realized the rancher was quite drunk. A profusion of small broken veins were fiery red across his nose and cheeks.

"I'm sorry 'bout this, Lashiter," Chandler said, the words slurred.

"It's my goddamn brother who's behind it!" Millie cried.

"I will have no wife of mine cussin'," Chandler said stiffly. A sloppy smile was stretched across his lips, but reddened eyes advised that the admonition hadn't been made in jest.

Men were pushing the crowd back so that a cleared space was formed in the big yard between the east side of the house and the main barn.

"Amigo, stand up to him!" Luis Herrera was yelling. Vaqueros joined in with shouts of encouragement, some of it in Spanish.

A scowling Lassiter felt himself being pushed toward the clearing where Brad Sanlee still stood on a heavy packing crate, his thick legs braced, wearing a malicious grin.

Lassiter broke away from those shoving at his back. He strode purposefully toward the big man on the box, saying, "It won't work, Sanlee."

"Let's see you get outta this one, Lassiter. It's your finish!" This was spoken so low that only those in the immediate vicinity heard it above the babble from onlookers. Brows were raised and glances exchanged.

But as Lassiter reached out for one of Sanlee's ankles, intending to pull him down from the packing case, lights exploded in his head. It came on the heels of a tremendous blow to his left rib cage, which forced the air out of his lungs. Breath came gushing out. Pain ripped across his chest. He saw the surprised faces of the crowd tilt first one way, then the other. And the earth itself was tipping. As he fought for balance, there was a second savage blow, this one aimed for the jaw. But at the last moment, instinct caused Lassiter to bring his head down sharply. Knuckes crashed instead against his forehead. For the second time, his skull was filled with a vision of Shorty Doane's scarred features wavering before his eyes.

"Duck, Lassiter, duck!" It was Luis Herrera shouting through cupped hands, the voice barely audible above the hubbub. Women were screaming as Doane waded in, his huge fists lifted for the kill. Even hurt as he was, Lassiter couldn't help but realize that the intention was for him not to leave this yard alive.

With his head buzzing strangely, Lassiter began backing, slowly at first, just barely keeping out of range of Doane's superior reach. Inevitably, Doane finally caught up with him. But at the last instant, Lassiter whipped his face out of range. He literally felt a blast of air as the mighty fist whipped past his ear. . . .

11

After backing once around the arena, with Doane stumbling after him like an enraged bear, Lassiter found that his head was clearing. And his arms no longer seemed weighted with heavy chains. He could breathe again without pain. He wondered vaguely if the tremendous blow to his side had splintered ribs. There was no time to worry about it now because he was fighting for his life. Brad Sanlee intended to see him stomped to death before this gathering of wedding celebrants. And there would be nothing done about it. The likely explanation to the law would be that Doane got a little overzealous in a fair fight—in case a sheriff was even interested. Sanlee's word would probably be accepted without further investigation.

"Brad, you had no right!" It was Millie's stricken voice. But in the uproar that followed, the rest of what she said was lost. Because Doane was charging again, coming with the force of a wild-eyed ladino straight out of the brush, both fists swinging. Still

Lassiter kept out of his reach, the blows whistling ominously just short of his nose, chin or mouth.

But suddenly Lassiter knew it was time to go on the offensive, if ever. Abruptly he whipped aside to send a left smashing into Doane's ribs. The big man, charging straight ahead, lost a step and his knees almost folded.

"A sample of what you gave me," Lassiter said through his teeth, and measured Doane's wide face. His right opened up a cheekbone. As blood spurted, his left found Doane flush on the mouth. Doane's head snapped back, surprise replacing a gloating triumph.

It was a late-nineteenth-century version of David and Goliath played before over a hundred spectators gathered in the yard, every man shouting, the women screaming. Several times the crowd was forced to back hurriedly when the combatants reeled from the cleared area.

When Lassiter paused for breath, his fists aching from hammering at the big man, he saw that his opponent's face was smeared with blood. But Lassiter had taken his own punishment. There was a sharp pain in his jaw and again it was hard to draw a deep breath.

Doane was coming on relentlessly when Lassiter brought him to his toes with a vicious uppercut. As Doane wavered, Lassiter heard a shouted warning at his back. And on the heels of it something crashed into his right shoulder.

"A bottle!" a man cried. "Somebody throwed a bottle!"

Brad Sanlee shouted indignantly, "We'll have none of that!" But he was grinning and nodded at the burly Joe Tige, who was edging back into the crowd. An empty whiskey bottle went bouncing across the yard, glittering in the harsh sunlight.

The pain came after the brutal impact of the bottle. Lassiter lurched and his right arm collapsed, lifeless as a strip of rolled-up carpet. With the useless arm dangling, completely numbed, Lassiter fought off the attacker with his left.

When Doane took a moment to smear a forearm across his bloodied face, Lassiter buried a left in the pit of his stomach. Doane lurched, both hands reaching out to clasp the tops of Lassiter's shoulders. Doane's weight was too much. Lassiter found himself slammed to the ground. In desperation, he tried to squirm out from under the great body that pinned him to earth. But he was trapped by two hundred and thirty-five pounds.

Blood from Doane's smashed nose splattered Lassiter's cheek. Doane was reaching up between their bodies with both hands, trying to get Lassiter by the throat. Before he could be strangled, Lassiter gave a mighty wrench of his body and managed to twist free from under the weight.

With the crowd cheering for him now, Lassiter staggered to his feet. Feeling had begun to return to his right arm. As he backed away from Doane, who was struggling up from the ground, he swung his arm in circles to restore the circulation. At last, knowing he had regained control of it, he began to hammer mercilessly at Doane's jaw and midriff. From a corner of his eye, he glimpsed a look of agony on Millie's sweet face. She stood with a small fist pressed against her lips.

And as Doane staggered and Lassiter swung

around to meet him head on, he saw Isobel Hartney at the edge of the noisy crowd. Her eyes were unusually wide with excitement, her red lips open.

Another blow from behind, this one just below the shoulder blades, bent Lassiter almost double. As his upper body whipped downward, he was met by Doane's uppercut—a blow so powerful that he was lifted off his feet and sent crashing to the ground. In his dimmed vision, Lassiter saw another bottle bouncing across the yard.

But, in the roaring from the crowd, he realized more protests were being uttered at the unfairness. And again Brad Sanlee echoed them. But a look of concern that had been growing on his bearded face, as Doane seemed to falter, was replaced by one of relief.

Doane was advancing on the prostrate Lassiter—a giant about to stomp a pygmy. As Doane drew back a booted foot near Lassiter's skull, most everyone felt that it was all over. There were sobbing protests from some of the women to stop it, but no one seemed to hear. Half the crowd screamed encouragement to Lassiter, but the rest seemed mute, frozen by the tragedy they were about to witness.

But at the last minute, Lassiter rose up from the ground. He caught the swinging leg with its boot toe that had been aimed at his temple. He clasped both hands around the leg and leaned on it with all his weight.

Doane screamed in pain and fell heavily on his back. Onlookers screeched. Taking a deep breath, Lassiter scrambled to his feet. Doane was getting up slowly, flexing the right leg that had taken the full weight of Lassiter's body. For a few moments a baffled look settled in what could still be seen of his eyes in puffy skin rapidly turning purple. Then all at once he seemed to snatch a revival of strength from the dusty air of the yard. He launched himself straight at Lassiter, obviously intending to end it.

"Time's up!" a voice cried. But no one paid any attention to Kilhaven at the table with a large gold watch that indicated the thirty minutes were up. His attempts to get the attention of the crowd were drowned out by a mighty roar. The two combatants stood toe to toe, slashing with fists at face and midsection.

"Stay away from him, amigo!" Herrera yelled to Lassiter.

But Lassiter knew he had to finish it. His knees were wobbly. His arms felt heavy as logs. But still he kept on. Then suddenly he was aware that Doane's blows lacked their former strength.

It was then he stepped back and struck twice at Doane's jaw. But he was dismayed when the big man failed to topple. There was nothing to do but pursue him doggedly. Again Lassiter slammed him on the jaw, then drove a wicked left and right into the softness above the broad belt buckle. A sheet of perspiration was jarred from Doane's lank hair. He lifted his face. He had lost a tooth. The gap showed through smashed lips. His mouth hung open as he staggered and gasped for breath. But Lassiter's uppercut snapped it shut. Doane's teeth slammed together with a click. All of Lassiter's waning strength had gone into that terrific smash to the jaw.

Doane took half a dozen staggering steps, his arms dangling at his sides. Then his eyes, in the mass of purplish flesh, turned upward. He collapsed.

Lassiter reeled away. Shouting men had him by the arms. They were hustling him over to a bench at the nearest of the outdoor tables. He slumped down when his weary legs gave way. A glass of whiskey was thrust under his nose. But he shook his head.

"Water . . . first," he gasped.

After drinking what seemed half a bucket from a yard pump, he reached for the glass of whiskey.

Doane's prostrate figure was ringed by the curious. Small boys stared in awe at the fallen gladiator and then at Lassiter on the bench, his long legs outthrust. One eye was nearly closed. His forehead was deeply gashed. And there was a cut on the point of his chin. He was breathing heavily.

Rep Chandler stood with an arm slung around the slim waist of his bride, looking dazed by it all. The excitement of his wedding, too much whiskey, then the tension of witnessing the monumental brawl between his new foreman and Shorty Doane had about done him in. He was breathing nearly as hard as Lassiter and had to sit down. His face was gray.

Millie looked at him with concern. "You all right, Rep?"

He nodded his head. "Fine, fine," he mumbled.

Then he levered himself to his feet and limped over to congratulate Lassiter.

Lassiter looked up at the rancher out of hard blue eyes. "Where's Sanlee?" he demanded softly.

"Gone. Him an' his men. Doane's layin' in the wagon that brought Millie."

"Too bad. I wanted to finish it with Sanlee. . . ."

"You ain't in no shape to stand up to him, Lassiter," Chandler pointed out. "Your hand's all swollen."

"Joe Tige's got my gun."

"Well, was I you, I wouldn't ask him for it," Chandler said. "I'll give you money to buy another. Tige can be mean."

Lassiter gave a hard laugh. He stood up and scanned the crowd to look for pinned-up pale hair and green eyes. "Maybe Isobel Hartney's stomach won't turn at sight of my face," he muttered.

Millie, standing next to him, said, "She went with Brad." Then Millie added, "Stay away from her. She's poison."

Millie was looking at him with concern in her eyes, or was it jealousy? In his condition, he couldn't be sure. But in the next instant he negated jealousy. Of course not. Hell, she was a bride and it was her wedding day.

After the historic battle, it was a subdued crowd that partook of the barbecue. Lassiter felt a great need for food and wolfed down two thick slabs of barbecued beef and a pound of beans. After numerous cups of black coffee laced with whiskey, he felt his strength returning.

Making sure no one saw him except Luis Herrera, whom he gave a signal by lifting his chin, he slipped away. Herrera's long dark face was grim as he found Lassiter waiting by the barn, away from the milling crowd.

"What is it, amigo?" he asked tensely.

"I need to borrow a gun. Tige took mine."

"Wherever you go, I go with you." The segundo started away, but Lassiter caught him by an arm.

"Just the gun, Luis," he said, looking into the black eyes.

Herrera blew out his breath, then hurried away. The guests were chattering among themselves near the tables. Dust kicked up during the fight had finally settled. The sky was Texas blue with only a fringe of dumpling clouds. A breeze had come up, cooling the air and carrying with it aromas from the barbecue pits.

The musicians were playing *El Niño,* and guests were soon pairing off to dance to the lively tune.

Herrera returned with a big .45 under his jacket. Gravely, he handed it over to Lassiter.

"You be careful," the Mexican hissed in Spanish. "Today the saints were on your shoulder. But perhaps not twice."

Lassiter smiled, clapped him on the back and went to saddle his horse. But because of his condition, Herrera helped him.

"Don't tell anybody about the gun or that I've gone," Lassiter warned from the saddle. And Herrera nodded that he understood, but still not liking it. He watched Lassiter take the town road and disappear into evening shadows.

Lassiter kept his black horse to a walk because the jolting punished his already aching body. There was no hurry. If Sanlee was doing what he thought he'd be doing, it would probably continue for most of the night. Faint moonlight turned the brush into ghostly gargoyles.

He wondered if he should give Sanlee time to put on his britches before he called him. Probably. He shouldn't be found bare-assed naked in the vacant lot next to the Hartney Store. It would shock the town ladies who would have been awakened by the late-night pistol fire.

When he finally saw the stark outlines of the store in night shadows, not a light showed downstairs nor in the windows of the second floor. Of course, Isobel Hartney being the modest soul she was wouldn't want lamplight shed on her activities of the night.

He gave a wry grin at the thought. Twisting his lips caused him pain and he swore softly.

He didn't know what color horse Sanlee had ridden away from Box C or whether he had ridden in a wagon. No horses were tied to the store's hitching racks. Of course, if Sanlee intended to spend the night, which he would, then his horse or wagon was no doubt at the livery stable. Over at O'Leary's on the far side of the street, the windows were still yellowed with lamplight. There were four horses at the rack in front.

He rode over and dismounted stiffly, looped the reins over O'Leary's tie rack, then ambled like a drunk through the swinging doors. A cowpuncher was slumped against the bar, his head down, singing nasally about his prairie rose.

The three other patrons were paying no attention, talking among themselves. The bartender this night had a body that reminded Lassiter of a bundle of slats tied with string. At sight of Lassiter coming through the door, his mouth fell open.

"What in hell happened to you?" he sang out.

"Somebody swung open a barn door just as I was goin' in," Lassiter told him with a laugh.

The singer broke off his song and looked around, as did the other customers. Lassiter stared at the four men, feeling disappointed he was so keyed up, that not a one of them was a Diamond Eight rider. In the strained silence that followed, with the men staring openly at his beaten face, he had two quick whiskeys. Throwing a coin on the bar, he then walked out in his stiff-legged stride.

"Gad, he looked like he just escaped from hell with the devil's pitchfork proddin' his ass," the barkeep breathed. "He had a look in his eye that freezes the gut."

"I know he froze mine," said the long-legged singer in dusty range clothes. "Who is he, anyhow?"

"Name of Lassiter. He works for Rep Chandler. There was a weddin' out there today. I wonder what Lassiter's doin' in town?"

"Well, whatever it is," said one of the drinkers, "I'm sure glad the reason ain't me."

Lassiter hammered on the rear door of the Hartney Store. "Miss Hartney, tell Sanlee I'll be waitin' for him in the lot next to your store!"

A dead silence followed. A faint breeze was blowing odors from the stable two blocks away. In the distance came a faint yip of coyotes. It woke up somebody's mule and it began to bray.

A window was lifted upstairs and a head with long, wheat-colored hair was thrust out. "Sanlee isn't here," she said in a loud whisper. "Wait and I'll be right down."

Two jolts of whiskey at O'Leary's in his condition had hit him hard. In a few minutes the rear door was unbolted. Isobel Hartney, wearing a green wrapper, stared in surprise at the shiny .45 pointed at her stomach.

Lassiter said, "Oh, I figured Sanlee might be right behind you."

"Come in, Lassiter." She stood aside. "And please put up the gun. I'd rather you didn't shoot me." He could see her white teeth in the gloom of the hallway. Her laughter was soft.

She stood aside while he debated. Then with a shrug, he stepped in and she closed the door. He stuck Herrera's gun in the belt of his trousers. She took his hand in warm fingers and led him toward a flight of stairs.

"Where's Sanlee?" he asked as he started to climb.

"Home, I expect."

"You left together. So I was told."

"He was in a frightful mood."

"I can imagine. He's the kind that hates to lose."

"And you presumed you'd find him here." They were at the top of the stairs. "You presume a lot, Mr. Lassiter."

"I only add up what I see with my eyes."

"Then your vision is faulty," she said lightly.

He was led to a spacious bedroom where she pushed him gently down on a bed with rumpled covers. The bed was warm from her body.

Then she knelt before him, tugging at one of his boots, and looked up into his swollen face. "With us, there's no preamble, Lassiter," she said. "No coyness of courtship."

She got one of his boots off. It thumped to the floor. Her voice tightened when she said, "Today you were magnificent. No Roman princess in ancient times ever longed for her gladiator as I longed for you today."

"You speak right out, don't you?"

"The academy for young ladies which I attended tried to teach us that we had an equal place in the world of men, and not to bury our desires." The second boot was off.

"Your parents didn't care about what you were learning?" he asked her smiling face.

"My father. Mother was gone long before him. Had he known, however, he would have yanked me out of that school by the hair of my head."

As she spoke of her school and the progressive headmistress, she was tugging at his clothing. And when at last he lay back on the bed, she touched him, saying in awe, "You're everything I imagined."

Part of the enjoyment of the night, he supposed, was the fact that he was driving a spike into Sanlee's pride. He didn't believe for a minute what she'd implied about him having an overactive imagination where she and the Diamond Eight owner were concerned.

"My horse," he said, rolling aside finally in sheer exhaustion.

"Stay where you are. I'll put it away for you."

Before he could protest, she was gone. His eyes closed and he was breathing heavily.

It seemed hours later that he felt her creep back into bed. He fell asleep again with her hand resting on him.

When he awoke again the experience was even more rewarding than before.

It was getting to be daylight and he could look down into her face and see lips faintly parted, the green eyes awash with contentment.

"I feel completely shattered," she said softly. "You're the best thing that has happened to me . . . ever."

Although she begged him to stay, he said it was impossible. For one thing, her clerks would soon be reporting for work, he pointed out, and it wouldn't be right to possibly expose her to gossip. Although he sensed there was probably already much of that where Sanlee was concerned.

"What would you have done if you'd found Brad last night?" she asked curiously as he was ready to leave. She was sitting up in bed, her arms wrapped around her knees, her long, pale hair loose at bare shoulders.

"Tried my best to kill him," Lassiter said shortly.

"That was a cruel trick he played on you."

"And you knew about it." He reminded her of their brief conversation prior to the fight.

"Brad told me he planned something—a drinking contest between the two of you was what I gathered. Well, I couldn't see any real harm in that, although I wanted to warn you to be on your guard. Brad can be tricky."

"Yeah. Good night, Isobel."

She laughed gaily. "Good morning, you mean. The most wonderful bright morning of my life. When will I see you again?"

"I'll be in." He kissed her and left.

By not being available last night, Brad Sanlee's life had quite possibly been spared—or Lassiter's spared, if Sanlee had proved to be faster on the draw. Lassiter thought about it as he rode home in the clear dawn light. Birds chirped in cottonwoods and huisache blossoms scented the air.

His experience with Isobel Hartney had cleared his mind, restored his body—at least to an extent. He found that he liked Isobel. At first he had considered her haughty, but she wasn't at all. In certain situations she was a tigress with velvet claws.

At least he was getting back at Sanlee. In one way it was evening things up for Vince Tevis. And eventually Sanlee would get wind of it and come looking for him. Then would come the time for wiping the slate clean for Vince Tevis.

Finish Sanlee—or be finished—whichever way the cards happened to fall on that day of violence that was to come. . . .

12

Millie lay in the big bed, staring at moving shadows on the ceiling made by the shifting cottonwood branches in the breeze that had come up after midnight. From the yard, there still came sounds of revelry. Men who seldom got together with neighbors were reluctant to cease the flow of whiskey which was a stimulus for talk. An argument was going on concerning the merits of Sam Houston. All too familiar, for Millie had heard it often when at last, upon the death of her mother, she had been moved to the big Sanlee house. Her late father had been a staunch supporter of Houston and anyone who held a differing view of the patriot of Texas was wearing the devil's forked tail.

As she lay in the darkness, wearing her bridal nightgown, she heard the arguments taper off and she thought, thank God.

But voices soon rose again. This time the subject was General Santa Anna de Lopez who had stormed the Alamo. But there was no argument there as everyone agreed. And the recollections became so heated that she was afraid that possibly the Anglo guests, so inflamed by alcohol and revived hatreds, would march to the bunkhouse to take out their anger on the vaqueros.

However, she was sure that Luis Herrera could handle the situation should it arise. She had known Luis since she was small, and knew him to be a generous, smiling man who could be dangerous if crossed. She felt more comfortable having him as a stable part of her new life as mistress of Box C than if he weren't on the payroll at all. She could count on him where she knew it was foolish to expect too much from Lassiter.

Vince Tevis had mentioned him several times, saying with a laugh that Lassiter could stay put just so long, then was off seeking new trails.

Ever since she had been trying to fall asleep, the name of Lassiter had periodically been rolling around inside her head. Many times during the past hours she had relived the violence of the day, always reaching the conclusion that Lassiter surely was an incredible man. He never gave up when the odds were so against him, even from the start because of Doane's great size and expertise in the business of bare-knuckle fighting. Obviously, what she had heard was true; her brother had hired Doane in the first place for his punishing fists.

Lassiter had withstood not only those fists but two thrown bottles that had certainly slowed him for a time. But on both occasions he had bounced back.

At last she heard the lurching footsteps of her new husband, singing under his breath as he cast off his clothes and climbed into bed. He mumbled something but she couldn't make out what it was.

She assumed it had something to do with now declaring his rights, as her mother used to call it with her nose in the air. Yet her mother had allowed Brad's father to treat her worse than a peon and had never fought back. Millie had secretly loathed the old man even though he had relented after her mother's death, and let her live under his roof. He had even sent her away to school, which was a mistake, he had ruefully admitted later. Because an education had put too many grand ideas into her young head, such as declaring the role of females was not ordained from birth at the direction of a father.

But by then he was old and too engrossed with other problems to exert a firm hand. As a result, she had done more or less as she pleased, to the consternation of the community.

During his lifetime, Poppa had kept Brad on a tight rein, but upon his death there was no longer a restraint. She knew that Brad planned for a cattle empire no matter how it was achieved, no matter how much blood was spilled. A tremor shot through her at the thought. She thought of Lassiter riding out this evening with such a cold look in his eye that it was frightening. She sensed he was going after Brad even though when she questioned Luis Herrera he was noncommittal.

"You cold?" her new husband asked thickly.

"No, Rep."

"You shivered."

"I . . . I guess I was a little cold."

"You need warmin' up."

She was surprised with all the whiskey he had consumed and the raw emotions stirred up that day by her brother's rash act that he seemed virile as a young bridegroom. She did her part, hoping to please.

And when he finally collapsed, a dead weight, he mumbled, "I want us to have a son. I ain't too old, am I?" There was such a plaintive note in his voice that it tore at her.

"Of course you're not, Rep."

He gave her a pat on the stomach, then turned awkwardly on his side because of the bad leg. Soon he was snoring.

The prospect of possibly bearing his child gave her no joy. And she knew it was wrong to feel that way. Had she done him a disservice, after all, in agreeing to the marriage? She only did it to shut Brad up. She knew it was cowardly to be afraid of one's own kin. But Brad had maneuvered her into this trap and now she would make the best of it. As she had told Lassiter, she would be a good wife to Rep Chandler. It was the very least she could do.

It was midmorning when from a parlor window she saw Lassiter riding in. He seemed more hunched in the saddle than usual and his face, what she could see of it under the low-pulled brim of his black hat, was a mass of bruises.

She went flying out to see him. "You're all right," she gasped when he dismounted.

He gave a crooked smile with his bruised mouth. "As well as could be expected, I reckon."

"You didn't run into Brad?" she asked tensely.

He hesitated and looked away. Even at midmorning, wagons of late sleepers were still rolling out of the yard. Rep had come out to shake the many hands and to wish everyone luck on the trip home.

"No, I didn't see Brad."

She blew out her breath. "Well, that's a relief."

He was still showing her that crooked grin which tore at her heart. And his blue eyes seemed to bore into her. Be careful, Millie, she warned herself. You're no longer fourteen and now you're a married woman.

"You look mighty well this mornin', Mrs. Chandler," he said.

It was the first time he had called her by her new name. She liked the way he said it. "Thank you, Lassiter. I wish I could say the same about you." They laughed together.

That afternoon he loafed around the home place. It gave her a chance to talk to him. But it became awkward when she tried to pry into his past life. He turned the subject to Vince Tevis.

"Vince said you and he were trying to find your aunt."

"We were. Aunt Marguerite, my mother's sister. But she'd moved from Las Cruces and I was told she'd gone to Ardon. But I don't know whether she was there or not. I never had a chance to find out. Brad came . . . and well, you know the rest."

Two days later Lassiter was in town with the Chandlers when he saw Joe Tige just crossing the street down the block. The burly Diamond Eight rider was about to enter the saddle shop when Lassiter stepped up. Tige looked surprised, then scowled.

Lassiter said, "I want my gun."

"I don't know what the hell you're talkin' about," Tige snarled. He started to step around him and enter the saddle shop, but Lassiter blocked him.

"The day of the wedding. You took my gun. I want it."

Drinkers had come out of O'Leary's across the street to stare at them. It crossed Lassiter's mind that some of them might be Diamond Eight. But at the moment he didn't give much of a damn if they were.

"You're crazy as hell," Tige blustered. "I never took no gun."

Lassiter's eyes finally lowered to the man's holster nestled against a thick thigh. He saw a familiar gun butt with black grips protruding from the leather.

"It's a good gun," Lassiter went on. "You must think so, too. You're wearin' it."

Tige looked at him for a moment, then his thick lips stretched tight in a grin. "Try an' take it. . . ."

That was as far as he got. The .45 borrowed from Herrera appeared in Lassiter's hand, the hammer eared back. Tige came to his toes, a look of surprise on his brutal face.

"Don't bother to hand it over," Lassiter said softly. "I'll just take it."

Ramming the muzzle of the cocked .45 against Tige's side, he reached out with his left hand and retrieved the .44.

Tige, muttering under his breath, entered the saddle shop and slammed the door. The owner, who had observed the incident through the fly-specked front window, was ashen-faced.

When Lassiter walked back to the Hartney Store where he had left his horse beside the Chandler wagon, the rancher came out to the loading platform and said, "What was that all about?"

"He borrowed my gun the other day. I wanted it back."

"When I saw you headin' for him, I kept my fingers crossed. Tige's got a hair-trigger temper. Let's go get us a drink. The missus, she's got some stuff she wants to buy. You know how women are. Can't make up their minds."

Chandler smiled and gave a playful tug at one end of his mustache. How easily Chandler was fitting into the role of husband, Lassiter thought. But then he'd had years of practice with his late wife.

Chandler stuck his head in the door and spoke to Millie, who was looking at yard goods by the strong light of a front window.

Isobel Hartney, a pencil behind her ear, stepped to the door. "You're looking some better, Lassiter, than you did the other day."

"Some," he agreed and looked at her. Today she wore a big apron and her yellow hair was parted in the center and drawn back severely from her pretty face and done up in a knot at the back. Her eyes were lively, her smile seductive, the way she kept running the tip of her tongue lovingly along the lower lip. Lassiter wondered if she'd seen Brad Sanlee. Probably.

"Rep's right about Tige," she said. "He has a nasty disposition. He won't like it that you relieved him of a gun, yours or not."

"I'll keep one eye open for him," Lassiter said. "And the other eye on more pleasant things." He gave her a direct look. Then, with a wave of the hand, he was walking with Chandler toward O'Leary's.

It was ten in the morning and this time of day there were only two other drinkers in the large saloon. A swamper was dismantling the big pot-bellied stove near the center of the room, cleaning out the winter buildup of soot. It wouldn't be used again till fall. Lassiter felt he would be long gone by then.

Chandler spoke in a heavy voice as he mentioned Brad Sanlee and poured whiskey for them. "Brad ain't foolin' me none," he said in a low voice. "I know that with me marryin' up with his kid sister that he figures to get a foot in the door at Box C."

Lassiter had told him as much before the wedding. But he didn't bring it up to Chandler. He savored the good whiskey, staring out a rear window at the unending miles of brush that stretched south from Santos.

Chandler said, "Well, Brad's got another think comin'. It's why I wanted a tough foreman like you."

Lassiter felt uncomfortable, sensing what was coming next. Chandler would outline the many reasons why he should stick around.

"In one way it's a good thing I busted my leg," the rancher was saying. He was waiting for Lassiter to say, "Why so?" But Lassiter remained silent.

"Bein' laid up with my leg gives me time to chew things over, Lassiter. I know damn well Brad had gone to hunt Millie down. An' knowin' Brad, I figured he'd bring her back sooner or later."

"And he sure did," Lassiter put in, thinking of Vince Tevis.

"I tell you, Lassiter, the fight you put up with that bastard Doane was one of the best examples of pure guts I ever did see. How you stood up to him I'll never know. But you sure did."

"I had no choice. Either stand up to him or have my skull busted like a dropped melon."

Chandler smiled at that, then grew serious. "I'm gonna do my damnedest to get Millie with child. I want a son so bad I can purely taste it."

That kind of talk about Millie was disturbing to Lassiter. He didn't like to think of Millie's sweet young body entwined with the creaking framework that housed the spirit of Rep Chandler. He wondered if Chandler at his age was still up to fathering an offspring.

"I need a son to carry on," Chandler said and started to refill Lassiter's glass.

But Lassiter put a hand over it. "I need a clear head in case Tige wants to start anything."

"Yeah." He refilled his own glass, then started talking again about a son. Then he seemed to descend into a black mood. "Likely, I won't be around to see him grow. But you will."

"Now wait a minute there. . . . That's years away and . . ."

But Chandler rode right over the objection he was about to voice. "I'm countin' on you, Lassiter. All the way."

"We'll see," was all that Lassiter felt like saying at the moment.

"A man with my years on his back oughta know better'n to try an' bust a mustang. But I did. That's where I got my busted leg. An' while I was layin' there thinkin', I got out the ranch books. Things kinda gone to hell since Bertha died. I ain't been payin' much attention. But it seems I owe a hell of a lot of money to a bank up at San Antone."

"You had a good cattle sale," Lassiter said, mentioning the $74,000 he had brought back from Tiempo.

"I reckon that'll help . . . some."

Lassiter didn't have time to dwell on it because he looked over his shoulder and saw Tige leave the saddle shop and start across the street toward O'Leary's. Lassiter tensed when the big man swaggered right up to the swinging doors. He was about to open them but peered over the tops and saw Lassiter. They locked eyes for a moment.

Then Tige said, "Be seein' you," in a threatening tone.

He wheeled from the double doors and stormed away, his boots rapping the boardwalk with such force it seemed he had a personal vendetta against the planks underfoot. He got his horse and headed down the street in the direction of Diamond Eight.

Chandler, oblivious to what had gone on, was talking about the years that stretched ahead. They would be good years, he said, with Millie having a bunch of kids to keep her happy. But again Lassiter reminded himself that he had no intention of being tied down for years on a Texas ranch deep in the brasada. Chandler would just have to understand when the day of parting was at hand.

But it seems that mortal men seldom realize fulfillment of the grand plans they have made. Rep Chandler was no exception. Tragedy's shadow began to loom ominously over the Texas brush country a week later.

Chandler was over east near the boundary of Kilhaven's Slash K when Brad Sanlee, mounted on a big grulla, rode out of a mesquite thicket. "Rep, I got somethin' to tell you," Sanlee said gravely. "Alone."

Chandler frowned a moment. Five of his vaqueros were accompanying him as they moved a small bunch of Box C cows to better grass. Chandler told them to go on ahead, that he'd catch up. Then he added, just to be on the safe side, in case Brad had any skullduggery up his sleeve, "If I ain't caught up to you in ten minutes, you come lookin' for me." A warning to Sanlee, just in case.

They looked from Chandler to Sanlee and nodded.

When they were again pushing the small herd, Sanlee said, "There was no need to do that, Rep. You act like I might do somethin' to you."

"What's on your mind, Brad?"

"Hell, we're kinfolks, you an' me. I'm your brother-in-law. You can't forget that." Sanlee sat with his big hands folded over the scuffed horn of his saddle. "I've been hearin' talk I don't like, Rep."

Chandler felt a stiffness in his shoulders. "What kind of talk?"

"Now it's between you an' me, Rep. She's my sister an' all that, but I feel obliged to look after my new brother-in-law. . . ."

"What in hell do you mean, Brad?" Chandler demanded coldly.

"It's talk I've been hearin' that I don't like."

"For Chris' sakes, get to the point!"

"It's about her an' Lassiter."

Chandler swallowed and turned his head to focus on a cluster of yellow blossoms against the green of the brush. "I don't want to hear another damn word, Brad." His voice shook. He gathered the reins in his left hand, preparing to ride on, his eyes raking Sanlee's bearded face.

"I'd keep my eyes open all the same. I know that sister of mine pretty damn well. I ought to. I grew up with her."

With that, he turned his grulla and galloped off, his wide shoulders tight in a Texas brush jacket, hat on the back of his head. It crossed Chandler's mind how easy it would be to put a bullet in that broad back and end that gutter talk. He hoped to God that Lassiter didn't get wind of it and go trying to avenge the Chandler family honor. He knew that

Lassiter thought a heap of Millie and she of him, which was only natural, Chandler told himself, as he began riding slowly through the brush to catch up with his men. He could hear the sounds of cattle trampling the brush as they were moved out. Sure, Millie liked Lassiter because he was her husband's foreman. Nothing more than that. Not one damn thing more than that.

When he got home late that afternoon he saw that Lassiter had finished up early. He was at the corral, standing straddle-legged, holding the end of a lead rope attached to the bridle of a small pinto. Aboard the pinto was Luis Herrera's ten-year-old nephew, who was on a visit. Lassiter was teaching him to ride bareback.

Looking on was Millie.

As Chandler reined in to watch the fun from a distance, the boy slipped sideways and was pitched off. Lassiter instantly snatched him from the ground. From what Rep could see of Millie, she was smiling broadly. She had both arms draped over a pole in the corral. Her black hair was in two braids hanging down her slender back. She looked like a young girl. Chandler's heart went out to her. But a moment later he froze as she groped between the corral bars and caught Lassiter by the hand. She said something to him and they both laughed.

Then she saw Chandler riding up. "You work hard today? I fix you a good supper." At times, he noticed, when she was excited about something, she took on the speech colorations of her late half-breed mother.

He swung down and one of the vaqueros took his horse. Millie slung an arm around his waist as they walked to the house together. "Lassiter was telling

Jaime that he should know how to ride bareback in case he is ever out someplace without a saddle. . . ."

"That's Herrera's job," Chandler interrupted. "To teach his nephew." He spoke so gruffly that Millie removed her arm and looked up at him with a frown. His mouth was a grim line under the mustache.

"How cold you sounded just then, Rep."

"What's for supper?"

Midway through the meal, she said off-handedly, "Lassiter's taking the big wagon to town tomorrow to pick up supplies. I thought I'd ride with him. I want to get some more yard goods to match the sample I got the other day. I think it's a lovely shade of blue. . . ." She broke off, staring through the light of double candles to Chandler's tight face. "Rep, what's the matter?"

"Nothin'," he said grumpily.

"But I . . ." She drew a deep breath. "You told me last night it would take three or four days to move cattle to where you want them. I just thought that as long as Lassiter was going to town anyway . . . and you said I shouldn't ride alone because of Brad . . ."

"Oh, no, you go ahead. I got somethin' caught in my throat for a minute is all." He coughed several times. "There, I got it down. Piece of gristle, I reckon." The smile he gave her was ghastly.

Millie frowned down at her plate and finally pushed it aside. My God, he didn't think that Lassiter . . . Today she had impulsively reached for Lassiter's hand because he was bringing so much pleasure to a young boy. Had Rep seen it?

She decided to bring the matter into the open. "Rep, don't be jealous of Lassiter."

"Now that's downright silly of you to say." His

laughter was strained. She spoke again of going to town.

"And I thought it would be a chance for me to get away from the account books. You asked me to go over them, you know."

"Yeah."

"Far as I can tell, most of the money from the cattle sale is already owed. Some bills are two or three years old, Rep."

"Yeah."

At first he had been on the verge of forbidding her to go to town with Lassiter. Then a small voice had said, Keep an eye on them. See what they're up to. . . .

But the next day Millie didn't go to town with Lassiter. She said she had a headache. So Chandler was surprised when he saw the wagon from a screen of brush, at the halfway point. Millie wasn't sharing the high seat with his foreman.

He rode back home, wondering.

When he got home, Millie was dragging around the kitchen with a long face. He asked her about the day and beamed when she told him she had decided not to go to town after all.

But the joy went out of him when she added, "I had a feeling you really didn't want me to go."

He spluttered and stammered for a moment, then managed to speak a straight string of words. "Now that's the craziest thing I ever heard of."

"Well, you certainly didn't act like it last night at supper."

"I didn't feel too good."

She looked at him critically. "Rep, you do look sort of peaked." And there was something in his eyes she didn't like and the corners of his mouth dropped. There seemed to be a grayness in his face.

She told him that he needed a bath and then she'd put him to bed. "You look like you might be coming down with the fevers. . . ."

"Naw, I ain't. All I got . . ." He hadn't planned to tell her, but since the wedding he'd felt an occasional sharp pain when he breathed. "Well, all I got is a mite of pain in my chest. Musta been from that piece of gristle I had a time swallowin' last night," he said, passing it off lightly.

By the end of the week she brought up another troubling subject. "*Every* night, Rep? You should rest up a day or so in between." She started to say, "A man your age . . ." Then she decided not to because it would puncture his vanity. All she said was, "I don't think it's good for you. Not every single night."

Somehow in all this intimate discussion the name of Lassiter crossed her mind. Her heart sang for a few moments, then she turned the feeling off like it was a spigot. "It's for your own good, Rep," she finished.

In going over the books, Millie found their affairs to be in deplorable shape—even worse than she imagined at first. Her husband hated keeping records and Herrera didn't understand it. And Vince Tevis, while he was foreman, had left it up to the boss.

Finally, after much hemming and hawing, Chandler admitted that his late wife had handled the books and kept everything running smoothly.

Most of the money from the cattle sale had gone in delinquent mortgage payments to a bank in San Antonio. It was agreed that Lassiter should take north another thousand head of cattle for a quick sale. They needed money.

"Could we go along, Rep?" Millie suggested. "It would be exciting."

Chandler scowled at his wife. Did she think something might happen to him on a cattle drive and she'd have Lassiter all to herself? Then he put the idea out of his mind, hating himself for even thinking it.

He told her they'd stay home. It was Lassiter's job to drive the herd. "When he gets back an' we're more or less squared around, we'll do some of that travelin' we talked about."

He kissed her. She was a sweet girl and he loved her dearly.

There was another reason for not going north. He just didn't feel up to it. What he needed was a change without work, to see new country, new faces. Most of all, he needed a long rest.

13

With summer coming on, the heat in the jungle of brush was more intense than it had been at the original roundup. This time they worked alone, with no other outfits to give them a hand.

It helped to minimize the hardship because the cattle had not drifted too far since roundup. Many times during the hectic days Lassiter asked himself how and why he had gotten into this. But it kept going back to that twilight in Ardon, New Mexico, the time of tragedy coming so unexpectedly in a reunion with Vince Tevis. He still hadn't settled the score with Sanlee, who had been keeping away from Box C. What he didn't know about were the outpourings into Rep Chandler's unwilling ear to build up the image of cuckold.

Lassiter intended to take seven men with him on the drive, leaving the rest—including Herrera—at Box C, in case Sanlee decided to move in during his absence.

Fortunately for Box C, the East, after a few dry

years, was hungry for Texas beef. Cattle prices were up and the railhead at Tiempo was booming.

Millie drove a buckboard out to the holding ground with her husband as passenger to watch the start of the northbound push. It was a warm day with only a few clouds speckling the blue dome of the sky.

When Lassiter had the herd on the move at last, the ornery cattle finally in line with the more docile animals and making their slow, mile-eating pace, he rode over to the buckboard. It was parked in the sparse shade of a towering mesquite. Lassiter whipped off his hat and scrubbed a sleeved forearm across his forehead.

"We're rolling." He gestured at the cloud of dust thrown skyward by animals on the move.

Chandler looked drawn, Lassiter noticed, and kept biting his lower lip.

"I drove today because Rep wasn't feeling too well," Millie explained. She patted her husband on the knee.

"I was gonna get one of the men to drive," Chandler said, his voice strangely tight, "but Millie insisted on comin' along to see you off."

Millie threw back her head and laughed; it was forced. "Of course I wanted to see Box C beef on the move. It's important to us."

"You got a big job ahead of you, Lassiter," Chandler put in with a weak smile, "but I know you can do it."

"It won't be easy, but what is?" Lassiter didn't like the tension he felt between the couple.

That day Millie wore a fawn-colored hat with a wide brim to shield her face from the sun. Her hair hung down her back in a single thick braid. Lassiter found himself wanting to reach out and touch it. He restrained the urge. She was watching him out of dark eyes as if reading his mind. The sleeves of a plain calico dress were pushed up on her rounded forearms.

"Just be careful, Lassiter," she said solemnly. "And keep an eye open for my dear brother." Her lips twisted.

"Not one eye but two," Lassiter said with a hard grin.

"I oughta be goin' along with you," Chandler said and stared morosely at the dust ballooning above the slow-moving herd. The buckboard team, a bay and a chestnut, flicked flies with their tails and occasionally stomped the ground restlessly. A row of vultures on a mesquite limb some distance away regarded them solemnly.

Lassiter wondered if they were an omen. He felt a chill.

Chandler produced a paper from his pocket and handed it to Lassiter. "Like before, here's my power of attorney," the rancher said, "so you can sell my cows an' collect for 'em."

And again Lassiter was heartened that Chandler trusted him so completely, at least so far as money was concerned because he was noting a return of tension between the newlyweds. And for some strange reason, a prickling at the back of his scalp told him that he was the cause of it.

"Anything else, Rep?" he asked in a level voice.

"Just get back soon as you can," Chandler said gravely. "We'll miss you . . . the both of us."

He put out his hand, which Lassiter shook.

Millie extended a slim right hand. "Good luck, Lassiter," she said solemnly, her eyes still fixed on his face. Her hand was so soft, the pressure of her fingers gentle in contrast to her husband's crushing grip. Lassiter found himself wondering if she really liked him. Or was it just that he was her husband's foreman and for now a source of money to keep the ranch operating? The latter was a much safer assumption than the first, he told himself.

But he couldn't help but be aware of the roundness of her figure barely outlined in the flowing dress. How loose ends of her dark hair curled around small ears, and the sparkle of her eyes behind thick lashes.

Then angrily, he cleared his mind. It was just that he was bone-weary from the rushed gathering of a herd that had allowed his thoughts to drift into such dangerous channels.

He lifted a hand to the man and woman, then wheeled his black horse and galloped off to catch up with the herd.

When Millie slapped the reins along the backs of the team and they were rolling toward the home place, Chandler said, "You hadn't oughta shake hands with him."

She turned in surprise. "Why not, for God's sake, Rep? I wanted to wish him luck. And the Lord knows he'll need it." She grew silent as the buckboard rattled and swayed along the wheel tracks through towering brush. "I worry what Brad may do next."

"Maybe Brad's on our side now."

"Why would you say a thing like that?" Then her black eyes grew hot. "Has he been talking to you?"

"Well . . ." Chandler's face, which seemed to be graying lately, started to redden.

"He *has!* Damn it, Rep, you should know better than to listen to Brad."

"I don't like you cussin' like a man."

"It's a small worry in face of what confronts us. If it hadn't been for Lassiter helping us go over the books, we'd be on our way to the poor house."

"Lassiter again."

"Sometimes lately you act like you despise him. What's gotten into you, Rep?"

"I see how you look at him sometimes."

"Oh, Christ . . ."

"There you go again, cussin'."

"Rep, listen to me." She was hunched over, the reins gripped in her slender hands. "I am your wife. I intend to remain your wife, your faithful wife, until the day one of us dies."

"You're hopin' it'll be me."

"How can you *say* that, Rep! How can you?"

For two miles they rode in silence, then Chandler put a hand on her leg. "I don't know what's got into me lately. Been feelin' kinda poorly an' I reckon it's made me think things that ain't there."

"Believe me, Rep, they're not there at all. Now I want you to go and see the doctor."

"Clayburn ain't fit to doctor horses, let alone humans."

"But he's all we have. When Lassiter gets back, let's go up to San Antone, if you don't have any faith in Doc Clayburn."

"I feel a heap better now. Gettin' it outta my system is what done it."

"Jealousy. Rep, I'd never have believed it of you."

"Gimme the reins. I'll drive." He was grinning. "Can't wait to get you home."

She turned over the reins and gave him a troubled smile.

* * *

Brad Sanlee called the six men around him. "The herd's headin' north. Pinto just brought word." He inclined his head at Pinto George who leaned his tall frame against the Diamond Eight barn. His hair and brows were almost albino white, his eyes so pale that sometimes it was hard to tell the iris from the whites.

Joe Tige said, "Well, let's get on the move then." He turned for his horse, but Sanlee called him back.

"Hear me out, Joe," the bearded Sanlee said roughly. "I don't want nothin' to go wrong this time." Enough had gone wrong in the past already. Deverax and Bolin failed to kill Lassiter in New Mexico. Then Krinkle and his cousin, the one with the nervous trigger finger, bungled things in Santos. And most humiliating of all, Shorty Doane at the wedding celebration failed to tromp Lassiter into the Texas earth. His hard gray eyes slid to Doane, who stood with heavy arms folded. At long last, his face was healing. But new scars had been added to the old. "Catch Lassiter an' his bunch in an ambush. I want that herd."

"Once we got it, then what?" Doane asked.

"Take it to Tiempo. Charlie Buckmaster will meet you an' take it off your hands."

"Won't we have to change the brands?" Tige wanted to know.

Sanlee smiled. "Buckmaster will take the herd off your hands. Do I have to tell you more?"

"Seems this Buckmaster must be a slicker packing-house rep," the burly Tige said with a laugh.

"The main thing is it'll break Chandler. My friend Hobart at the bank says he's the same as walkin' a thin rope over a deep canyon."

The six men smiled at that. Besides Doane and

Tige and George, the other three were Chuck Hale, Dave Rance and Jeddy Quine. All of them were hired on Diamond Eight not only for their ability with cattle but mostly for a proficiency with weapons. It was hard for Sanlee to realize that Lassiter had already cost him Bolin and Krinkle. And Deverax was still hobbling about and likely would never be a whole man again.

Sanlee gave more details of how he wanted the matter of Lassiter and the herd handled. It prompted a question from Jeddy Quine. He was all bone and scant flesh, tall as the others, with the exception of Doane. The lid of his left eye had a habit of closing partway when he was under stress.

"With Lassiter out of it, how come you don't just move onto Box C without bustin' Chandler?"

"Because I want to bring my dear sister to her knees," Sanlee snarled. "Now go on, get the hell out of here." He stomped away, then wheeled and leveled his thick forefinger. "An' when you come back, bring me good news. You hear?"

The six men nodded.

Sanlee went to the house, where he started to pour whiskey into a glass, then changed his mind and gulped from the bottle. Elva Dowd, using a feather duster, looked disapproving. He ignored her. His hand shook as he lifted the bottle a second time. The stupid questions that brought Millie into it had set him off. Millie, goddamn her to hell! Then tears formed in the corners of his eyes—tears of rage and frustration. When the old man had brought her home to live with them, Brad had fallen wildly in love. And because she was no longer a kid, the old man had noticed it. One day the old man yanked Brad out to the barn. He wet a catch rope in a rain barrel, doubled it and used the rope viciously on his son.

"She's your *sister!* Don't you to your dyin' day ever forget that! If you touch her, you'll burn in hell for a thousand years! You hear me, Brad? And worse, I'll beat every square inch of hide off your miserable body."

Brad, bleeding, could barely stand. The old man threw the reddened rope on the barn floor and snarled, "Today was only a sample!"

Brad Sanlee had heard every word and aside from killing his own father outright, knew the threat would always be hanging over his head. To this day, he still bore the scars across his back and buttocks. But even though at times since the beating he was tormented almost beyond endurance, the old man's warning had been embedded in his brain as if chiseled in granite. One thing had been settled: If he couldn't have Millie himself, then by God, he'd at least dictate whom she married.

A second drink calmed him. With Chandler broke, Millie would have to run to her big brother and beg. Sanlee would finally pat her on the cheek and give them enough to live on. From the way Rep was looking these days, Sanlee didn't think he'd last long, broke or not. Who was next? he wondered. Why not Kilhaven? He owned the largest of the three spreads east of Box C. Mrs. Marcus Kilhaven. Millie should be pleased. It had a nice sound to it.

From the window he saw his men riding out. "Good-bye, Lassiter," he said aloud and lifted his bottle high in a toast of death to the enemy.

14

For three days Lassiter sensed that someone was stalking them. Time and again he would leave point and ride to the drag, the tail end of the herd where dust boiled and stung the eyes. There he would scout their back trail. It was flat country, crisscrossed by deep gulleys, and always a distant wall of brush on all sides. On cattle drives north, first to Kansas, then the shorter ones to advancing railheads, a wide swath had been trampled through the brush by thousands of big Chihuahua steers that had passed this way.

On the late afternoon of the fourth day, he rode back a mile to settle his suspicious mind once and for all that they were being trailed. This time he was rewarded. He saw no men, but spotted the tracks of six horses.

His heartbeat quickened as he drew his rifle and looked around. Where the horses had halted were cigarette butts scattered about and one half-smoked cigar. It was still faintly warm against the back of his hand.

Quickly he ran in circles to pick up the sign again. He found it to the west, beyond a stretch of caprock where hoofprints didn't show. Tracks led down into a deep canyon that paralleled the route being taken by the herd.

Running back to his horse, he vaulted into the saddle and started at a gallop to catch up to the herd. His horse had taken only a few lunging strides at this tag end of a dying day, when the faint crackle of distant rifle fire stiffened his spine.

He rode hard, wind searing his eyes, making them tear. As he came within sight of the herd, spread out across flat country, he saw no sign of strange horsemen. There was no tangle of brush to obstruct his view, just barren ground. It had been his intention to push on until reaching the grass he remembered from the previous trail drive.

It was like a tableau he beheld, every one of the thousand head of cattle standing tensed as if statues carved from reddish wood, topped with a forest of great horns. When there was no further firing, he began to wonder.

He slowed his horse because a hard-running animal could send the herd into the scourge of all cattle drives. *Stampede!*

Lassiter fired a question at a slender rider named Leon Monjosa.

"Rafael thinks he sees riders." And Monjosa gave a great sweep of his arm to the west. Rafael Guiterrez had fired his rifle. Others had joined in. But so far as was known, they had hit nothing.

"There are riders over that way, for sure," Lassiter

said. Monjosa stiffened and peered to the west where the sky was acquiring long streamers of reds and yellows as the sinking sun was hidden behind a cloud bank. There was no water or grass. Slowly, Lassiter circled the herd and cautioned the other vaqueros about firing at shadows.

"Wait till we run into the real thing," he told each of them.

Alert for trouble, Lassiter rode at point, peering tensely ahead into the growing shadows. He knew, as well as he knew that the day was Tuesday, that there were horsemen out there somewhere. And instinct told him they were the enemy.

Shorty Doane had appointed himself boss of the group. And because of his enormous size, none of the others protested. Even Pinto George, who had a waspish temper, let it pass.

In a deep canyon where shadows already were thick, Doane turned in the saddle of his big Morgan. It was the only horse available that could support his weight over long distances.

"I want Lassiter for myself," he announced.

"What'll you do when you get him?" the bony Jeddy Quine asked slyly.

"Aim to use this." Doane slapped at the bone handle of a knife that had been jammed into his boot top. "When I get tired of playin' with him, I'll cut his throat."

"Been thinkin'," Chuck Hale mused, "why didn't Brad come along with us?"

Joe Tige rubbed the back of his hand across a nose that had once been broken. "Yeah, I wonder about that. Brad's so all-fired set to put Lassiter under. You'd think he'd want a hand in it himself."

"The boss has got other things on his mind," Doane snapped.

They were riding single file along the bottom of the narrow canyon. Scrub cedars jutted from sand walls. Doane finally told them that he was going to have a look and started up a long, slanting trail that led to the highlands above. "Watch for my signal," he warned.

The lip of the bluff was well screened with brush, so he felt he would be protected. Besides, he knew the area well, having helped trap a small band of Comanches suspected of stealing horses when he was in the cavalry. Later, they had learned the Indians were innocent, but by that time it was too late. Doane and three other troopers had been kicked out of the service for taking the law into their own hands, instead of bringing the Comanches in as ordered.

As a result of that experience, Doane hated the cavalry almost as much as he did the law in general, which he had flaunted for some years.

His horse moved quietly in deep sand up the slanted trail. At last he reached the lip of a bluff and through thick brush saw the approaching herd. It was about a quarter of a mile away. There was still enough daylight to reveal Lassiter's tall, erect figure at point. Doane grinned. Perfect.

He turned in the saddle and gave an arm wave to those waiting below. Immediately, they started climbing the trail. Doane waited impatiently until the last man was riding up. They sat in their saddles, watching the approaching herd through the screen of brush. The animals were close enough now so they could hear the click of touching horns, the muffled sound of many hooves on the hard-packed earth.

A full moon to the east was dim now but taking on color as the world began to slide toward darkness. The west was ablaze with rainbow colors and the first star winked against drifting clouds.

"Each one of you pick a man," Doane hissed to the group gathered around him and now peering at the herd that was less than fifty yards away. "If Lassiter even looks like trouble, I'll shoot his horse. Then I'll have the bastard. Let 'em get a little closer."

From the tracks he had followed for a ways, some miles back, Lassiter knew there were six riders. He was hoping to reach water and grass before the riders made their move. He was under no illusions; they weren't just riding to see the countryside.

He had already sent the chuck wagon on ahead so a fire would be laid and food cooking by the time they arrived at Cedar Creek, the spot chosen for the campsite. By now the lumbering chuck wagon was only a hundred yards away. If he could only get the herd onto decent grass, he thought.

With full bellies, they would be less inclined to run if startled. But at best they were unpredictable, Lassiter well knew. He had hoped to make it to Tiempo without incident; only one more day would do it. They had been on the trail just under two weeks. He felt a tautness across his shoulders that so often was a prelude to disaster.

He rode with his rifle across his thigh, scanning the shadowy terrain ahead. His hand was slick with sweat on the metal. There was a coldness in his gut. Two of his men rode at swing on either side of the herd. Monjosa was still at drag with another man. And he had a man driving the chuck wagon.

Lassiter had just turned his head right for a long

scan ahead, swinging it left. Where thick brush bulged at the lip of a canyon he saw something move. He was lifting himself in the stirrups for a look down into the canyon. It was already in shadow. But his eyes snapped back to the movement. He squinted, his heart pounding.

Then he saw it again, plainly this time. It was the crown of a hat he saw, a tall man in the saddle of a big horse, he judged from the height.

He was just lifting his rifle when a man sang out, "Grab the sky, Lassiter! You're covered!" It sounded like the booming voice of Shorty Doane.

Instead of obeying the command, Lassiter spun his horse. An orange-red wink of flame appeared in the brush. And to the right, just behind his position of a moment before, a huge steer reared up on its hind legs, uttering an unearthly bellow. Blood streamed from a hole in its neck. Then it crashed to the ground. Other rifles were opening up. A man screamed, then uttered a Spanish oath.

Lassiter fired at the spot where he had seen the hat crown, but there was no answering cry of pain. It had all taken no more than four seconds. Suddenly there was a roaring, as if the earth itself was shaking loose. One moment the cattle were maintaining their plodding walk, but with the sudden death of the big bull in their midst, they were running. The ground shook from the awesome roar of hooves pounding the hardpan, the sound like that made by a hundred loaded ore wagons at runaway speed down a steep mountain grade.

Lassiter danced his horse away from a phalanx of leaders. They swept past, but a great wave of reddish-brown hides was roaring toward him. He spurred the black horse into a gallop.

"All right, you bastards!" he yelled at those in the brush. He put the shoulder of his hard-running horse into the side of a big lead bull with a bunch of speeding followers at his heels. Finally he was able to turn the lumbering animal and held his breath until certain that the others followed. They sped straight for the area where he had spotted the movement of the hat crown. A man yelled a warning. "They're comin' right for us!"

It ended in a hoarse scream as the leaders, heads down, plunged through the brush and disappeared over the lip of the canyon. A cacophony of bellows followed as doomed cattle plunged to the rocks below, probably twenty or thirty head of beef in the bunch Lassiter had peeled off from the main body of the stampeding herd.

Now he was swinging back in front of the oncoming storm of maddened cattle. It was either that or be swept over the edge himself. But he was barely able to keep ahead of the front runners. And as he leaned over the neck of the speeding horse he prayed there would be no rodent holes that could snap a leg. Lassiter well knew that if he were thrown, it would only be a matter of seconds before he was pulverized by the flashing hooves.

On and on they raced, with Lassiter in the lead. Gouts of lather from the mouth of his valiant horse struck his face. He glanced back. It was if a great moving wall was seeking to engulf him. A forest of clicking horns bearing down. To his horror, he saw the chuck wagon overtaken. It disappeared from sight.

A lead cow stumbled, its hind quarters flipping into the air. Instantly five others roared into it before the herd parted, animals flashing past the pileup on either side.

Looking back, he saw Tony Buscar on the right flanks, flogging his Spanish pony with the reins to gain more speed.

After what seemed like an hour, the animals began to tire. The stampede was slowing, thank God. Lassiter, his mouth dry, gauged their speed and at the right moment waved an arm overhead and made a pushing gesture.

Buscar understood. And between the two of them they gradually turned the herd, pushing the weary leaders into an ever-tightening circle. They finally halted, tongues lolling, their sides heaving. Only then did Lassiter draw an easy breath. His hat hung on his back by a chin strap. He was coated with dust. His horse stood straddle-legged.

He saw two more of his men, Guiterrez and Monjosa, who had helped to get the herd circling until the stampede was halted.

"Where are the others?" Lassiter asked hoarsely, dreading the answer.

Monjosa reported that from his position at drag he had seen one or two of them cut down by rifle fire from brush by the canyon edge.

"Sanlee, sure as hell," Lassiter said angrily. "I recognized Doane's voice."

They pushed the tired herd on another half mile to Cedar Creek. It was now full dark, but the moon was up. By then, Alex Rinaldo had appeared, which meant three were missing.

Leaving his men with the castle, Lassiter retraced the two miles or so the herd had run. He didn't know whether any of Sanlee's bunch had survived or not when he had turned a segment of the raging herd into the brush that hid them.

Upon reaching the spot, he found that the thick brush had been chewed off at ground level by the flailing hooves as if by a giant machete. He peered over the lip of the canyon and could barely make out the bodies of twenty-five or so dead cattle. But because of deep shadows out of reach of the climbing moon, he couldn't tell whether there were horses and riders among them. The only chance any of them would have had was to flee down a slanting trail he could see, far enough to escape the avalanche of flesh.

Where the stampede had started, he found one of his men, shot through the head. It was Bricido Maldonado.

"Lassiter?" a voice called weakly.

"Yeah, it's Lassiter." He led his horse over to Rudy Ruiz, who had a bullet hole in his thigh. Lassiter tore off his own shirt and used it to plug the bullet wound and tied it in place with the sleeves. With Ruiz hopping on one leg, he managed to get him onto the rump of the black horse. The Mexican's mount was gone—God alone knew where—probably smashed into the ground.

One man was unaccounted for. He found him a few minutes later, unrecognizable as a human body. Who was still missing? He was so weary he couldn't even think straight. All he could think of was Sanlee, beating in his brain like an Apache war drum. By process of elimination, he realized the man trampled to death by the herd was Eddie Rios. He had been driving the chuck wagon. Yesterday he had sprained an ankle and to give it a rest, Lassiter had pulled Monjosa off the chuck wagon and given the job to

Rios. By such a trick of fate, Monjosa lived and Rios was dead.

Nearby he came to the pulverized chuck wagon, the team also unrecognizable as once-living creatures on God's green earth. The last Lassiter had seen of the chuck wagon was Rios standing up in spite of his bad ankle, like a charioteer, urging the racing team to top speed. But the next minute everything had been engulfed. He had heard nothing above the roar of the cattle. But there must have been screams of agony as Rios went down.

It was one more score to settle with Sanlee. One more.

All they had for supper that night and breakfast the following morning was jerky.

There was no trouble from the herd, for they were completely spent. But there was always the chance that Sanlee's men would make another attempt. Lassiter set out guards, each of them taking turns. But there was no trouble. Lassiter had one hope: that the cattle storming over the cliff edge had carried every Sanlee man to the canyon floor.

The next day he and Monjosa rode back to the ruins of the chuck wagon. With a bent shovel found in the wreckage, they dug a grave for Rios and Maldonado. A quick tally showed they had lost forty-five head of beef in the stampede, counting the one that had been shot when Lassiter spun his horse out of danger.

It was a grim Box C crew that, short-handed, drove the herd onto the holding grounds at Tiempo a day and a half later. There Lassiter collected for the cattle and then told Sheriff Doak Palmer about the herd being jumped. Palmer, a tall red-faced man with an

Adam's apple big as a knuckle, gave Lassiter a sour look when Brad Sanlee was mentioned.

"But you got no proof," the sheriff said, his thumbs hooked in the pockets of a green vest. Cattle cars were being shunted onto a siding with a great clatter of couplings.

"I heard Shorty Doane's voice," Lassiter said, beginning to feel heat in his face. "And Doane works for Sanlee."

"I can say for a fact that Brad Sanlee is one of our most respected citizens of Tiempo County," Doak Palmer said in his drawling voice. "I knew his daddy well. Brad wouldn't be a party to such a dirty business as you claim."

"Well, he was."

"I've heard of you, Lassiter. While you're in my jurisdiction, I'd watch where I stepped and keep my mouth closed."

The sheriff's flinty eyes bored into Lassiter's face. But Lassiter met him with his hard blue gaze, and in the ensuing strained silence the sheriff flushed and looked away.

Lassiter was so angered at Rep Chandler for letting his affairs get in such a mess that an additional cattle drive had been necessary, he used some of the proceeds from the sale to buy a team and wagon. It was to haul the wounded Rudy Ruiz back to the ranch.

"I hope on the way we run into those Sanlee sons of bitches," he snarled. "Nothing I'd like better than to heat up my trigger finger on the lot of 'em!"

15

High-heeled cowman's boots were not designed for hiking. After several hobbling miles, blisters began to form on the feet of the weary men. They were four Diamond Eight survivors of an attempted ambush.

Shorty Doane had to call a halt. He lowered his immense frame on a flat rock and pulled off his oversized boots. Pinto George was in a sour mood. His pale eyes were reddened; brows and hair that showed from under his hat, usually almost white, were now darkened from dust that had been blowing along the canyon floor. A stiff wind had come up, hurling sand into their faces. Jeddy Quine swore. Joe Tige scowled and said nothing. The four men spat grit and cleansed their mouths at a sluggish stream. All had been limping badly the past hour.

Jeddy Quine's left eyelid dropped almost closed as he turned on Doane. "You had Lassiter dead to rights. Why the hell didn't you kill him?"

"'Cause I wanted him alive," Doane snapped.

"An' it cost us Hale an' Rance an' put us afoot," Quine complained.

"You're alive," Doane snarled. "So shut up!"

Quine started to bristle, but Pinto George grabbed him by an arm and shook his head.

The burly Joe Tige had borne up on the long hike through the canyon better than the others. His yellowish eyes flicked over his three suffering companions.

"What we need is horses."

Doane agreed. Looking back, he still couldn't believe the disaster that had struck them like a bolt of lightning. One minute Lassiter was sitting in his saddle in plain sight—a perfect target—and the next his horse was suddenly wheeling. And the shot intended for Lassiter's arm, to bring him down, had struck a bull instead. And on the heels of the rifle shot and the bull's scream of pain, the herd stampeded.

In those few seconds, Doane saw some of the herd leaders shunted toward the great clumps of brush that hid the Diamond Eight men at the top of the long, slanting trail. The next thing Doane remembered were maddened steers plunging headlong into the brush. He barely had time to fling himself from the saddle. He landed at the top of the trail that was some two feet below the actual lip of the canyon. However, it provided just enough clearance so that the cattle, in their senseless charge, leaped over his prostrate body instead of grinding it to sausage. Their momentum swept his horse with them to the canyon floor. Tige, Quine and George had already dismounted, shoving their rifle barrels through the screen of brush to take aim at the two swing riders on that side of the herd. But after getting off two shots, killing one, wounding another, the herd was running. They just had time enough to follow Doane's lead by flattening themselves below the rise of ground as the runaway cattle cleared their bodies.

Chuck Hale and Dave Rance, who were still in the saddle, frantically tried to turn their horses in the narrow trail, but had no chance. Doane remembered their screams of terror above the thunder of the stampede as they were swept off the trail as if by a giant's hand. And with them went the rest of the horses, upended as they fell, legs futilely thrashing air as if that would ease the cruelty of the rocks below.

"Where's the nearest ranch in this goddamn country?" Doane demanded. "Anybody know?"

"Old man Harkness has got a place fifteen miles south of here an' over west," Pinto George grunted.

"Fifteen? Whyn't you say a hundred an' be done with it?"

"I been around here since I was a kid," George went on. "It's the only spread I know of in these parts."

Swearing at their bad luck, they bathed their aching feet in the stream, put on socks and boots and resumed their painful hike.

It wasn't until nearly sundown of the following day that they came in sight of the Harkness place. Ben Harkness had been at the place for twenty years. When he moved in, he was the only settler within fifty miles. He had surrounded his house with a wall built of rocks from a nearby creekbed, to keep out prowling Kiowa and Comanche. But after marrying a Kiowa squaw, they had mostly let him alone. His wife died two years ago and was buried on a knoll behind the house of rock and adobe. He ran a small herd of cattle and kept a few good horses on hand.

He was just filling a bucket from the yard pump when he happened to look through the open gate. He saw four men approaching. They were afoot, which was odd, and limping badly. His first impression was that they had been wounded in a gunfight. The big one had his teeth bared as if it was agony to take one more step.

Harkness went into the house and got his old Sharps. He levered in a .50-caliber shell and waited till they got near enough to hear his voice.

"What do you want here?" he demanded loudly.

Doane shouted through cupped hands. "Need horses."

"You got money?"

"Some."

Harkness sniffed at the word "some." "I can only let you have one. An' it'll cost you."

The men had halted some twenty-five yards away. Now they exchanged glances.

"We'll come ahead an' dicker," Doane called. They started walking again.

"Only one of you come," Harkness shouted back. "I want one hundred dollars for the horse."

"You go to hell, you ol' skinflint!" Doane yelled.

For an answer, Harkness sent one of the .50-caliber bullets whistling just above their heads. They halted abruptly.

"You got a hundred dollars between you?" Harkness called.

"Yeah," Doane replied after a slight hesitation.

"Looks like you'll have to take turns in the saddle. But it can't be helped. One horse is all I can spare." Harkness pointed to Jeddy Quine, whom he considered the less dangerous. "You come with the money. The rest of you stay put."

Doane, in a low voice, said, "Pretend we're diggin' money from our pockets. Then you take care of him, Jeddy. We need four horses, an' we ain't got all day to argue about it."

Quine made a great show of stuffing money into his pocket, then started forward. But Harkness yelled for him to leave his gun. Quine nodded and handed his revolver to Doane. Then he pretended to stumble. As he came up, he had plucked the bone-handled knife from Doane's boot. With the blade up his shirt sleeve, he started again toward the house. Its roof line could barely be seen above the rock wall.

As Quine approached, Harkness thought of letting Chief out of the house. He was a smooth-coated brown animal of enormous size but these days was unpredictable due to old age. But if the four men gave him any trouble, he'd turn Chief loose. They'd be limping a lot worse than they were now after Chief snapped at their legs and ankles a few times.

Harkness waited by the gate, a lean, weathered figure with a deeply lined face. He had the Sharps under one arm and an eye on the pocket where he thought Quine had shoved the money.

"Hand over the money first," Harkness ordered when Quine reached the gate. "Then I'll show you the horse."

"Sure," Quine said. Excitement made his left eyelid droop.

He shoved his left hand into his pants pocket, withdrew it slowly. Harkness had his greedy eyes fixed on the pocket. Too late he saw Quine leap. Quine brushed aside the Sharps and in the same movement his knife flashed. A stream of pinkish blood erupted from the seamed brown throat. Harkness collapsed, his blood staining the ground.

Quine waved the others in. "Looks like we got us four horses!"

A dog in the house was making a great racket, jumping against the front door and snarling.

"Better take care of it, one of you," Doane said as he hurried to the corral, as fast as sore feet would allow.

Just as he reached the corral, there was the crash of a .45. The dog no longer uttered a sound.

"We better get the hell out as fast as we can," Tige said.

Pinto George turned on Quine. "Did you have to *kill* him?"

Quine rested a hand on his gun and just looked at him.

"My pa brung me by a few times when I was a kid," George went on. "Harkness had his squaw give us supper a time or two."

"Bet your pa paid good money," Doane said with a harsh laugh. "Now quit your whining, Pinto. An' let's put miles between us an' this place."

Just in case they'd run into somebody who would spot the Harkness T Bar brand on the horses, they kept off the main cattle trail. They made a wide circle to reach Diamond Eight headquarters by a route where a chance meeting with anyone would be minimized.

It was midday when they came riding into the yard. A team and buckboard waited in front of the rather ornate ranch house, sunlight sparkling on wide front windows. The team stood with heads down, lines wrapped around an iron tie boy.

Brad saw them from a parlor window and stiffened in his armchair. Seated on a sofa, wearing a silk dress to match her eyes, was Isobel Hartney. Her long legs were crossed and she was regarding Sanlee out of narrowed green eyes. She said, "I'll have to give marriage a lot of thought, Brad. . . ."

He twisted in his chair to glare at her, his lips in the bearded face compressed to a pair of white lines. "You was more or less sure. Till that Lassiter showed up."

That caused her to smile. "Don't tell me you have spies in my bedroom." She knew instantly it had been the wrong thing to say, even in jest. He sprang out of the chair and his backhand swung. It struck her so hard that lights danced in her head. As she fell over on the sofa, he went storming out the door. She heard him thumping down the veranda stairs, yelling stridently, "Where're the others? What in hell *happened!*"

Most of her life, she had been aware of his explosive temper, so why had she goaded him? Her face throbbed. She sat up and gingerly felt her right cheek. There would be swelling and quite possibly a black eye. It crossed her mind to tell Lassiter what Brad had done. But just as quickly she tossed the idea aside. It would mean the end of Lassiter, no matter how valiant he might be. Brad would crush him with superior numbers.

Out in the yard, Sanlee was listening to Doane relate the tragic incident. But he embellished the story. On the way, Lassiter had picked up more men and Diamond Eight was simply outnumbered, implying that Brad should have sent more men.

In the next breath, Doane told him about the horses and old man Harkness. "We better get rid of the horses, Brad."

"Yeah. In case somebody comes lookin' at brands." Then he rubbed his bearded chin. "Tell you what, hide 'em for a spell till I do some thinkin' on the subject." He grinned, then sobered. "Now I got to go to town." He loped for the house, knowing that after having her face punched, Isobel wouldn't stay the night.

He guessed he shouldn't have hit her. So far, during courtship, he had kept himself under control. Time enough to use the flat of his hand after the marriage vows were sealed. He recalled the old man blackening the eyes of Millie's mother a time or two. He supposed it ran in the family.

In the house, Mrs. Elva Dowd's austere features were expressionless, but she had evidently overheard the business with Isobel. He made his apologies to the green-eyed beauty while she listened stiffly on the sofa, her knees pressed primly together. The puffy right side of her face was an ugly shade of red.

"When I saw my four men come ridin' in as if nothing had happened, when I sent six to do a job, I . . . well, I just exploded. I'm sorry, Isobel, damn sorry."

"You may drive me home, Brad," she said coolly.

All the way to town he tried to make amends but she failed to respond. She just sat hunched in the wagon, staring at the miles of brush as if counting each clump.

At the rear door of the store he tried to help her down. But she alighted from the wagon without his assistance. "When'll I see you again?" he asked, standing with his hat in hand, a lock of coarse, reddish hair hanging over one eye.

"I'll let you know. I tripped over something is how I'll explain my face."

"Jesus, I'm sorry about that." Then he looked at

her intently, the eyes with their sheen of gray steel. "It ain't true about Lassiter, is it?"

Not wishing to risk his wrath twice in one day, even if now in town and at her own doorstep, she said, "Now that's the silliest thing you've ever asked me."

Giving him a faint smile, she hurried into the store. He heard her on the stairs to the second-floor living quarters.

It was a moment before he put on his hat. He stood there, a big man with shoulders tensed, thinking. Had there been just a flicker of something in her green eyes at the mention of Lassiter's name? Well, Lassiter wouldn't be alive much longer to worry about it. After they were married, he'd ask Isobel point-blank about Lassiter. And if he figured she was lying, she'd end up with more than a puffy cheek.

Jerking down the brim of his hat, he drove the buckboard over to O'Leary's and stormed inside for a drink from his private bottle. He was in such a mood that O'Leary, with his plump red face, kept out of the way.

Sanlee thought of his great plans that had somehow gone awry, thanks to Lassiter. When his father had died, instead of sorrow he had felt a great relief, a surging excitement that at last he was his own man to carve out his own empire. The old man had acquired Diamond Eight but had let that be the extent of his ambition. Not so the son. Brad Sanlee had a vision of owning a goodly share of acreage and cows in this part of Texas. All that stood in his way were Rep Chandler, Marcus Kilhaven, Rooney and Tate. With their acreage and cattle added to his, he could dictate his own terms, more or less, as to shipping costs and cattle prices. Year by year the railroad would be getting closer. It would cause the Santos country to boom. Sanlee was already making plans to be ready for it.

A lot of his current problems he laid at the doorstep of his sister Millie—her running off with Vince Tevis, Sanlee having to go tearing after her, wasting all that time trying to track her down, then the long trip back home.

And then that day he had seen Lassiter standing at the bar in O'Leary's and had offered him a proposition. How was he to know that Lassiter and Vince Tevis had been friends? And that Lassiter had actually come all this way looking for somebody named Sam Lee, which turned out to be Brad Sanlee in person. All this he learned from Isobel Hartney one lazy night when she was in a talkative mood and disclosed what Rep Chandler had told her in the store during the week.

And thanks to Shorty Doane and the other five pulling some brainless stunt, Lassiter still lived. But not for long. He poured himself another drink, his thoughts now focused on the horses stolen from a dead man far out on the lonely flats somewhere between Santos and Tiempo.

He actually smiled, which gave O'Leary the courage to smooth down his thinning locks and waddle up to ask Brad how things were going.

"Just fine," Sanlee replied with a hard grin. "Damn fine."

16

Lassiter didn't expect the reception he received at Box C when he rode in with the remains of his crew, Rudy Ruiz lying in the bed of the new wagon purchased in Tiempo. Lassiter was just swinging into the yard by the big barn when Rep Chandler staggered out of the house, waving a revolver.

"I figured you'd keep right on goin'," Chandler said in a thick voice. His sparse brown hair stood on end and there was a stubble of gray whiskers on his chin. His eyes were reddened and he smelled as if dipped in a vat of whiskey.

"Why would I keep on going?" Lassiter made himself speak calmly. Monjosa and the others eyed Chandler and the pistol.

"You come back for her is the only answer!" Chandler shouted.

"Who the hell are you talking about?" Although Lassiter knew, it caused all the tensions of past days to well up and trip his temper.

"My wife, that's who I'm talkin' about!"

The men were drifting to the bunkhouse, those who had been on the ill-fated cattle drive and the ones who had been left behind, wanting to get away from the loud voices and the accusations. Herrera looked narrowly at the drunken Rep Chandler.

Millie came flying from the house, her long black hair streaming. Tired and upset as he was, Lassiter couldn't help but notice how her clothing was pressed tight against her body, revealing every curve. Her dark eyes were filled with sparks.

"Rep, you fool you!" she screamed at her husband.

Chandler turned, blinking as she came up and took the gun from his hand. Millie was breathing hard, her bosom heaving. "Brad's been talking to him," she gasped, out of breath. "Putting . . . ideas into his head!"

Chandler sagged. He looked at Ruiz, who was being carried by two of the men. "What happened to him?" Chandler asked in a weak voice.

Lassiter told him, making it brief. He handed over a bank draft. Chandler squinted at it, then looked at Lassiter. "Why didn't you bring cash, like before? You know I trust you."

"Trust me?" Lassiter gave a harsh laugh.

"Don't pay no mind to me. I'm sorry, Lassiter. I been drinkin' too much an' when I saw you, somethin' exploded in my head."

Lassiter only shrugged. But his mind was made up for sure this time. He was through at Box C.

Chandler rested a hand on Lassiter's shoulder. All the anger had evaporated, leaving only a husk. "You'll take supper with me an' the missus tonight, eh?"

Lassiter nodded reluctantly and watched Chandler stagger off toward the house. He wished mightily that Millie had gone with him and not compounded an already ugly situation. But she stayed where she was, holding the pistol in both small hands.

"I'm sorry, Lassiter, really sorry. But worry over money and the awful things my goddamned brother whispered to him . . ." Tears danced in her eyes as her body trembled. "How could Brad be so . . . so despicable?"

"I want you to get Rep sobered up. Pour the black coffee into him before supper. I've got something to tell him."

In the wild run from the house, her hair had fallen across her face. Pushing it back, she peered at Lassiter. "You're going to leave," she guessed.

"It's best. Herrera can run things for you. He's a good man."

"I know he is, but . . ." Tears spilled down her cheeks. She rubbed them away with a smooth forearm.

He gave her a gentle shove toward the house. "Go on, Millicent. Don't make things any worse than they are."

"You remembered how I like that name. It sounded so sweet when you said it. . . ." Her lower lip trembled. "Oh, damn, damn, why are we put on this earth to suffer?"

"You made your bed like I made mine. You're married and I'm a drifter. It's high time I moved along."

"I'll miss you, Lassiter." Millie choked up and started away. "See you at supper." Then she was hurrying across the yard, her shoulders straight, long black hair touched by sunlight.

A grim Herrera came up to listen to Lassiter's account of the tragic twilight near Cedar Creek.

Lassiter was just putting on his clothes in the bunkhouse after a bath when he heard Millie scream his name. He rushed from the bunkhouse, not even taking time to put on his gun rig, but carrying the holstered weapon, the long belt flapping at each step. He found Chandler lying on the parlor floor. His face was gray and he was trying to sit up.

Millie was white-faced. "He was standing there and the next thing I knew he . . . he just fell."

Lassiter buckled on his gun rig while Millie spoke. Then he picked Chandler up, surprised at how light the man was, and carried him to the bedroom. Millie pulled down the covers. Lassiter laid Rep on the bed.

Chandler's eyes were open. "Hell, I'm all right," he said with a weak smile. "Was kinda dizzy is all."

Lassiter got Millie aside. "I'm going to send one of the men to town for the doc."

"I'd better go," a shaken Millie said, untying her apron. "Doc is a strange one. If one of the men came for him, he might take his time, or not come at all, depending on what kind of mood he's in."

"Hell of a doctor."

"He's all we have. He was out here the other day and he and Rep played poker. They did a lot of drinking and Doc shouldn't. He shouldn't even touch it and he knows better. So he . . . he may not be over it yet."

She started for the door, but Lassiter caught her. "I'll fetch Doc Clayburn. He'll come. Believe me on that."

But after the ride to town, it took nearly an hour to get the doctor ready to set a saddle. He had eaten—Lassiter had seen to that—for the first time in over two days: three eggs, a steak and biscuits at the Santos Cafe.

"The curse of mankind, strong drink," the doctor sighed when they were well out of Santos, cantering, his medical bag bouncing behind the saddle. "Rep's been having troubles so I tried to cheer him up. By doing so, I put another dent in my own soul. In my liver I guess would be a better way to put it." Clayburn gave a sour laugh.

"Rep's got nothing to worry about now," Lassiter said. It was late afternoon with the sun dipping into fleecy clouds and starting to stain them in rainbow colors. "I brought back enough money from Tiempo to see him squared away."

"Well, it wasn't altogether money that was troubling Rep." Then the doctor broke off and rubbed his chin and stared at a wall of mesquite they were passing.

"Go ahead and say it, Doc," Lassiter snapped.

"It . . . it's only gossip, I'm sure."

"Thanks to Brad Sanlee." Lassiter spoke the name with such venom that Doc Clayburn jerked around in the saddle to stare. He was slender in leg and torso but had a well-rounded stomach. To fill out his narrow face, he wore enormous brown sideburns.

The rest of the ride was made in silence. When they rode in, the vaqueros were kneeling in front of the main house. With them was Herrera's wife, a black rebozo over her head. Lassiter turned cold, thinking of Millie. "My God," he groaned.

They had laid Chandler out on his own bed. Millie stood woodenly beside it.

"I went to take him some broth and . . . and he was gone." Her chin trembled.

They left the room while Doc Clayburn made a brief examination. Then the doctor came to the parlor and slumped to a sofa. "Rep had a lot of things on his mind. I guess his old heart just pumped itself to death."

Millie sat in a straight chair across from him. She gripped her knees so hard the knuckles were white. "My brother did this to Rep," she said in a tight voice. "Just as surely as if he had used a gun."

"Don't upset yourself, Millie . . . Mrs. Chandler," the doctor advised dryly. "It's over and done. You can't help your husband now."

Millie glared through the moisture that clouded her dark eyes. "I know what you're thinking, Doc, and it's wrong, wrong. No, I didn't love Rep. But I respected him. And I would have made him a good wife. Isn't that true, Lassiter?"

"Very true," he replied gravely.

Doc Clayburn suggested they have a drink in memory of the late Jeremiah Rep Chandler. Millie got out Rep's bottle and poured into three glasses with a shaking hand.

"It's not proper for me to drink my whiskey straight," she said, her face stained with tears, "but at the moment I don't feel very ladylike."

Doc Clayburn drank so many toasts to the memory of the departed rancher that he was forced to spend the night. He slept on a spare cot in Lassiter's quarters.

In the morning, Lassiter made a silent ride with him back to Santos where arrangements were made for the funeral.

They buried Chandler in the ranch graveyard a quarter of a mile beyond the house, among the graves of vaqueros and ranch hands and next to that of his late wife.

Most of Santos had come out to pay respects to their neighbor. Kilhaven, Tate and Rooney were present with some of their men. The tall Kilhaven, the only one who had never married, stood alone.

There being no reverend in Santos and no time to send for one, Millie read from the Book of Psalms in a strong, clear voice.

Isobel Hartney worked her way through the assemblage to reach Lassiter's side. He saw her, stunning in black, her green eyes under pale brows slightly mocking.

"An attractive young widow and a ranch for the taking," she whispered. "What an opportunity."

Lassiter gave her such a cold look that she blanched.

"I . . . I was only jesting," she said quickly and touched his arm. But he drew away.

In the next moment he heard Sanlee's voice. "Sorry I'm late, sis, but . . ."

Millie was just throwing the first clod of dirt, thumping down onto her husband's coffin. At the sound of her brother's voice, she whirled, her black eyes alive with hatred.

"Get off this ranch, Brad. How *dare* you come here after what you've done?"

Sanlee, big and bearded, in a black suit a little too tight for him, clenched his teeth. "What the hell have I done?"

"You know, you *know!*" she cried, leveling a slim forefinger at her half-brother. "Get off this ranch. Or so help me God, I'll kill you myself!"

With his face flaming around the beard, Sanlee

stalked away. Some of his men had ridden over with him—Doane, Pinto George, Quine and Tige.

As they all mounted up, Doane turned his large skull and looked directly at Lassiter. There was no emotion on his scarred face, but his eyes were threatening. Then they all rode away.

Lassiter realized he would have to postpone his leave-taking until Millie got herself in hand.

17

With Rep Chandler's death, five of the vaqueros quit. They had liked working for Rep Chandler but didn't fancy being bossed by a woman, his widow. It was a matter of stubborn male pride. Luis Herrera had tried to argue, but they were adamant. Shortly after their departure, a drifter named Pete Barkley came out to the ranch asking for work. He was rangy and had a pleasant smile. But there was a hard, calculating look in his light gray eyes when he thought no one was observing him.

Herrera asked Lassiter if he should hire him on. Lassiter, with other things on his mind, told him to use his own judgment. Lassiter was trying to figure out some way to leave Box C without hurting Millie too much. Before quitting the country, however, he intended to have it out with her half-brother. Hopefully, it would be the elimination of Sanlee, not Lassiter. In which case, she would have a clear field to pick and choose her own way through life. He would make a suggestion—to give some favorable attention to Marcus Kilhaven. Kilhaven had told him once how much he admired her. At the time, Lassiter had sensed the feeling went a little deeper than simple admiration.

Two days after the Chandler funeral, Sheriff Doak Palmer rode to Box C with some grim-looking men. With him were Sanlee and Doane, the latter wearing a hard smile. Two of the sheriff's six men, all strangers from Tiempo, had a pair of loose horses on lead ropes.

"These was found in your pasture, Lassiter," Sheriff Palmer said, gesturing at the horses.

"Who found them?" Lassiter demanded.

"Don't make no difference." Palmer's flinty eyes were triumphant. "Brand belonged to a man named Harkness. Way I figure it, you needed horses after your herd stampeded an' killed a few. So you helped yourself to Harkness horses."

"Lassiter a horse thief?" Millie cried, coming to the yard in time to hear the last. "Impossible!"

"Sorry, Mrs. Chandler," the tall sheriff smirked. "Not only horse-stealin', but murder. Harkness was found with his throat cut."

"Oh, my God," Millie gasped.

"First off, my deputy figured Harkness, bein' a mean ol' cuss, had cheated one hombre too many. But then he noticed the old man's dog was shot, an' horses missin'. Horses found on your property, Mrs. Chandler."

"I simply don't believe that," she cried.

"I ask again, who found them?" Lassiter's eyes drilled the faces of Sanlee and Doane in turn. The word "murder" hung over the yard like a storm cloud. When it was obvious the sheriff wasn't going to answer his question, Lassiter said, "Let me get the men who were with me on the cattle drive. They'll swear we needed no horses."

The sheriff glanced at Sanlee from under his hat brim. Sanlee shrugged, as if to say, "Let him go ahead. Won't do him any good."

By then, everyone was dismounted, standing under cottonwoods beside the big barn.

In broken English the wounded Ruiz and the others swore that they had sufficient horses to see them through, even after the stampede.

"Proves nothing," Sheriff Palmer said indignantly. "Reckon I got to take you to the county seat an' lock you up, Lassiter. Till we sort this all out."

"Wait a minute, Sheriff," Lassiter said, his voice deadly calm, the cold blue eyes boring into Sanlee's face. "I can take you to the scene of the stampede, which was started by an ambush."

"What ambush you talkin' about?" the sheriff demanded.

"I'm talking about Diamond Eight."

And when Sanlee started to make an angry protest, one of the sheriff's men, gray-bearded and paunchy, said, "Doak, why don't you let him finish tellin' it?" Others in the party nodded in agreement. Sheriff Palmer looked irritated.

"Speak your piece, Lassiter. Then we got to get movin'."

"Along the lip of a canyon you can see where the brush is cut clean," Lassiter said. "The herd did that. The string of cows that I shunted away from the main herd."

"What about it?" Palmer demanded.

"They went headlong through that brush. And

right into the men hiding there. They swept some of the men into the canyon. I'll bet on that. Not only men but every horse."

Lassiter was gambling because Doane was getting fidgety, glancing first at Sanlee, then at Lassiter, his large, scarred face reddening in anger.

"Your word only, Lassiter," Sheriff Palmer said, plainly upset.

"I'll bet a hundred dollars against two bits that if we dig deep enough under what's left of those dead cows, we'll find horses. And they'll be wearing the Diamond Eight brand."

All eyes including the sheriff's turned to Sanlee and Doane. Sanlee bristled at such an accusation being hurled at him. But he kept his mouth shut. But Doane opened his. Obviously flustered and angered, trying to squirm out of the hole Lassiter had dug for him, the big man shouted, "So you admit turnin' them goddamn cows on us. You killed Rance an' Hale an' put us afoot."

In the dead silence that followed, Lassiter said, "Afoot?"

Sanlee gave the hulking giant a withering look. The sheriff seemed embarrassed.

"One way to settle it, Doak," said Ab Hunter, the bearded man who had spoken up before, "is to do like Lassiter says. Have a look at that canyon."

Sheriff Doak Palmer cleared his throat. "That won't be necessary," he said pompously. "The Harkness horses weren't actually found on Box C, but close to it. Close enough for me to be suspicious." He managed to give Lassiter a hard look. "We'll be ridin' on, but was I you, I'd watch which side of the hill I walked on."

When they had gone, Lassiter said, "It'd be nice if

the sheriff followed up on this. But I don't figure he will."

"It'll be a snowy day in July before Sheriff Palmer ever moves against Diamond Eight," Millie said bitterly.

It was a familiar story—a powerful rancher, a greedy sheriff. He wondered if they were too bright, either one of them. Or Doane, for that matter.

But he wasn't fooled. He recalled the look Doane had flung him the day of the funeral. He thought of Sanlee calmly writing out the names of the three ranchers he wanted Lassiter to gun down. Deadly as a cornered rattler was the way he assessed Sanlee, brains or not. Today the rancher had been made to look like a fool in front of others, thanks to Doane's imbecilic outburst. Sanlee wouldn't soon forget this day. And if Lassiter knew his man, the final move would soon be made. . . .

Rep Chandler had endorsed the bank draft Lassiter had brought back from Tiempo but never cashed it. The following day, Millie went to town to take care of it. But she returned looking angry and worried.

"Hobart refused to honor it," she told Lassiter stiffly. "He said there seemed to be something irregular about it. But he didn't bother to explain."

Lassiter remembered the banker well. Arthur Hobart, put together as if with three spheres: round legs, round belly and a head that reminded Lassiter of a large pumpkin.

"Arthur Hobart is beholden to Brad, I suppose is the explanation," Millie went on in a desperate voice. "We need that money to keep us going till next spring."

"Brad Sanlee again, eh?" Lassiter's face was cold.

"Do you want to ride in with me, Millie? I aim to have a talk with Mr. Hobart."

"I think it's hopeless. He says I'll have to go all the way to Tiempo to have the bank there honor it. But he says because of the irregularities, whatever that means, it may take weeks."

"I'll go to Santos alone," Lassiter said. "Want to give me the bank draft?"

She dug around in her blue reticule, found it and handed it over, then slumped to the sofa and stared out a window at the dusty ranch yard. "What can go wrong next?" She sounded despondent.

"I'll either bring back cash or see that it's credited to your bank account."

"Just be careful," she called to him, but he was already out the door and striding toward the corral.

As he hitched a team to Rep Chandler's hack wagon, he felt in his bones that the showdown with Sanlee was drawing ever nearer. This latest business with the bank only gave it another nudge. No doubt Sanlee had put Hobart up to refusing to honor the check.

He was taking the hack wagon just in case he decided to bring back cash; it would be easier to carry. He hadn't quite made up his mind yet.

When Lassiter entered the bank that afternoon, the only person he saw was a cadaverous clerk named Alan Johnson. He was perched on his high stool behind a wicket, wearing a visor, white shirt and sleeve guards. He didn't look up.

Lassiter said he'd like to speak to Arthur Hobart.

Johnson muttered, "He ain't in."

The door to Hobart's office was closed. Probably the banker had seen him coming along the walk, Lassiter reasoned. After taking care of bank business, Lassiter intended to go to the Hartney Store, where he had left the team and wagon, in order to buy the makin's. Yesterday he had used his last paper and emptied the tobacco sack. Millie suggested he might as well use what Rep had been using. Lassiter didn't mind drinking a dead man's whiskey, but he had an aversion to smoking his tobacco rolled in papers he had left behind on the good earth. Besides making a purchase, he hoped to see Isobel. After all that had happened on the Tiempo trail and afterward with the sheriff, he felt the need to see a pretty face. Not that Millie wasn't pretty, but with her it was different. She was Rep Chandler's widow.

A sign on the closed door said A. Hobart, President. Lassiter said, "I think Hobart's in there. Mind knocking to see?"

"Ain't in, I tell you." Johnson's bony fingers clenched a pen stuck in an inkwell.

"I think I'll take a look."

"You ain't allowed back there," Johnson cried in alarm.

But Lassiter had already stepped through a wicket. He was approaching the office door when it was flung open. Arthur Hobart loomed up in the opening, his eyes in the round skull blazing with indignation.

"I suspect you've come on behalf of that Chandler woman," he began, but Lassiter cut him off coldly.

He flashed the bank draft before his eyes. "I want the money. Now."

"You can't come in my bank in a high-handed way and expect . . ."

"You're taking advantage of the lady because she's a widow. And as her foreman, I don't figure to put up with it."

Something in the cold, clipped tones, the chill in Lassiter's eyes, drained Hobart's round face. His mouth sagged. He looked wildly out the front window in the direction of O'Leary's as if willing Brad Sanlee to step from the saloon and come to his rescue.

Lassiter smiled thinly, guessing what went through the banker's mind. "Might be all to the good if Sanlee did step up," he said, still in that voice that cut like an ax through ice. "We could finish up our business once and for all."

Hobart rubbed a hand over his mouth and reached out for the bank draft. But Lassiter shook his head. "Not till I see the money—$37,000."

"I . . . I don't have that much in the safe."

"Let's both of us go see if you've got it."

Johnson was still huddled on his high stool, his pen scratching as he pretended to work on the books. He looked around once, his eyes fearful, then returned to his task.

"You should go in for bank robbery, Lassiter," Hobart said with a shudder. "You'd be good at it. The way you look at a man freezes the spine."

"This isn't robbing a bank," Lassiter pointed out. "This is taking what is due the widow Chandler. As her foreman, I'm collecting for the lady."

Hobart unlocked his squat black safe, then spun a dial. He opened the double doors. Lassiter could see stacks of silver coins. Gold coins were in racks of various sizes depending on their denomination.

"Why didn't you honor the draft for Mrs. Chandler?" Lassiter demanded. "It would have saved everybody a lot of time."

"I . . . I thought it didn't look quite right. I was busy at the time and only glanced at it." Pouches under his hazel eyes were glossy with sweat. "I . . . I suggest you deposit the draft to the Chandler account."

"With your tie to Brad Sanlee, we'll take cash."

Hobart made a great show of indignation, puffing out his chest above his round belly. "See here, Lassiter, I treat every customer the same. And I have no more ties with Mr. Sanlee than with anyone else."

"We'll still take cash."

"When Chandler became hard-pressed after his first wife died and wanted a loan on his place, he went to a bank in San Antonio instead of me."

"I don't know anything about that."

"And now I'm supposed to kowtow to his widow. . . ."

With a shaking hand, Hobart counted out $37,000 in neat stacks on the table. Then he got a canvas bag, filled it with the money and pulled the drawstrings.

Lassiter picked up the heavy sack and stood, eyeing Hobart. He had no use for most bankers because they so often preyed upon the ignorant and helpless. This banker he detested. Hobart was a sneak; it was written on the pudgy face, the loose-lipped mouth, the eyes set in deep sockets.

Lassiter said, "You write a few lines for me, saying you gave me the money in good faith in exchange for a bank draft. Just in case you get ideas about claiming I took it by force."

"I . . . I've never been so insulted in my life."

Lassiter handed him a pen from an inkwell. "Write!"

Drops of sweat from the banker's face dotted the paper as he wrote what Lassiter instructed. It smeared some of the ink, but not enough to make it illegible.

When it was done, Lassiter folded the paper and put it in his pocket. Then he picked up the sack of money and backed to the door, with Hobart watching him nervously.

As he started walking toward the Hartney Store, Lassiter glanced over at the saloon, almost wishing some of the Diamond Eight bunch would be there and see him with the money sack. And try to take it.

Then he caught himself. No, that wouldn't be right. That money belonged to Millie Chandler and he had no right to place it in jeopardy.

All the way back to the store, he turned it over in his mind. He was still thinking about it when he put the money sack under the wagon seat and covered it with gunny sacks. Then he entered the store, standing at the front counter where he could keep one eye on the wagon through a window. The store was fairly crowded. Finally, Lassiter got the attention of a thin-faced clerk and bought papers and tobacco. Then he casually inquired if the owner was in.

"Miss Hartney went out to Diamond Eight. Brad is having a shindig. Important people that has something to do with the railroad is the way I heard it." He hurried away to wait on another customer.

"Wasn't meant to be," Lassiter muttered under his breath.

Then he stiffened. So she was out at Diamond Eight. Perhaps it was just as well that the hoped-for interlude had not happened after all. Just how far could he trust her? And he had the Chandler money.

As he stepped from the store, rolling a cigarette with the new tobacco and papers, he stared at the lump made by the money against the covering of gunny sacks. For some minutes a strong hunch had been coldly pricking the back of his neck. And he suddenly decided to act on it. He returned quickly to the bank, the money sack swinging from a long arm.

Upon seeing him, the bank clerk stopped scratching figures in a ledger. His eyes bugged out. This time Hobart's office door was open. Lassiter could see the banker at his desk, a sheaf of papers in his hand. Hobart's moon face was tense and white as he stared at Lassiter.

"Changed my mind," Lassiter announced. "With me havin' the money, there might be too much temptation for somebody."

He saw the surprise in Hobart's eyes. "But you *can't!*" Perspiration glistened at Hobart's hairline.

As yet, the bank draft had not been placed in the safe. With trembling hands, Hobart dug under some papers on his desk until it was uncovered. "It seems that you changed your mind very suddenly, Lassiter," he said hoarsely.

Lassiter upended the sack on the desk. A cascade of coins made a great clatter. "I got to thinking how foolish I've been," Lassiter was saying, "risking Mrs. Chandler's money."

"I don't know what you mean." Hobart was counting the money with jerky motions of his hands, his face set.

"Somebody could try and rob me on the way back to Box C," Lassiter said. And when Hobart's head snapped up, he read the truth in the vindictive hazel eyes.

When the money count was ascertained and the coins locked in the safe, the amount was added to the Chandler account. Lassiter made sure of that.

Then he had Hobart write another receipt to show that the money had been credited to Box C.

Only then did he take his leave from the fuming banker. . . .

18

The minute Lassiter left the bank, Hobart flew out a rear door and hurried across the street to O'Leary's. Plainly agitated, he entered the saloon and called O'Leary away from his bar.

"Has the man left yet?" Hobart demanded in a low voice. "The one taking my note to Sanlee, I mean."

"Well on his way by now."

"I want another man," Hobart said hastily. "Give me a pencil and paper, if you will."

O'Leary hurried to oblige. Then Hobart sat at an empty deal table and scribbled a hasty note. "Sudden change of plans," he wrote. "Will explain. H."

He folded the note, dug a five-dollar gold piece from his pocket and handed it to O'Leary. "Pick a good man."

O'Leary nodded and signaled a bandy-legged little man with a pock-marked face. He whispered to him, then gave him the folded paper. The five-dollar gold piece brightened the man's eyes.

"Ride like the wind," Hobart ordered.

As Hobart crossed back for the bank, he cursed the day he had allowed himself to become involved in Brad Sanlee's machinations. Everything had started to go wrong the day Sanlee, in a rage, had gone after his runaway half-sister and inadvertently brought Lassiter onto the scene. . . .

In the yard before the imposing two-story headquarters at Diamond Eight were saddle horses and several rigs of various descriptions. An azure sky was pitted with occasional lumps of white clouds. A breeze carried strong odors from the corral.

The bandy-legged rider, Tuck McReynolds, came pounding into the yard, causing some agitation among the horses tethered there. He thumped up the veranda steps and banged on the front door. From inside the house came a murmur of voices and laughter. They were suddenly stilled. The front door was flung open by a dour older woman.

"What do you want?" Elva Dowd demanded in frosty tones.

McReynolds told her that he had to see Brad Sanlee on a very important matter. The woman looked him over, then said, "Wait."

She went back into the house.

After the interruption when someone pounded on the door, Sanlee resumed a discussion concerning the railroad. His coarse, reddish hair was slicked down with pomade. He wore a brown suit, freshly ironed, a snowy shirt and string tie. His boots bore a high polish. He was a picture of the successful Texas rancher. The four men he faced were from San Antonio and had come all this way to hear Sanlee expound on his growing cattle empire.

"My poor sister, recently widowed as you know, has asked me to handle her affairs at Box C. So that means more acreage, more cattle added to the pot." Sanlee smiled around the thin cigar he was smoking and leaned forward in a leather chair. "It wouldn't surprise me at all if Kilhaven doesn't go in with us. After a suitable period of mourning, I expect him to ask for my sister's hand."

The four men in stiff collars and business suits exchanged glances and looked pleased.

"That leaves only Tate and Rooney on your eastern flank," said Luther Barnes of the Texas Central Railroad.

"Only a matter of time till they'll be in the fold," Sanlee assured them.

"Well, if you can guarantee the railroad that much business," spoke up Hector Landeau of the Great Lakes Bank of Chicago, "it makes sense to swing the tracks south from Tiempo instead of east. . . ."

Sanlee suddenly realized that Mrs. Dowd was at his elbow. He was about to tell her to go away, that he was discussing important business, but she leaned over, whispered in his ear, gestured at the front door and then departed stiffly from the room.

"Excuse me, gentlemen," Sanlee said heavily and started for the door. In the adjoining sitting room, which was his late mother's favorite gathering place, were several women chattering away, wives of the four men and of other guests.

As Sanlee strode for the door, Isobel Hartney stepped from behind some heavy red plush drapes and made as if she had just entered from the veranda by a side glass door.

With her blond head high, she strolled in the direction taken by Sanlee. Each of the four men straightened up to stare at her voluptuous figure outlined in fashionable silk.

On the veranda, Sanlee was scowling at a slip of paper McReynolds had handed him. Sanlee crumpled the paper and smiled. "It won't make no difference," he said, slipping back into the speech patterns of the range. "The main thing is that Lassiter bastard. . . ."

He broke off upon realizing Isobel stood nearby, her green eyes flashing fire. "I thought you was with the ladies," he snapped.

McReynolds scooted down the steps and hurried to his sweated horse. He had ridden hard to bring the note to Sanlee—a note about as important, it seemed, as a handful of dust in a high wind. Sanlee hadn't been a damned bit interested.

"Brad, I heard Lassiter's name mentioned," Isobel said crisply, stepping to the veranda and closing the door at her back.

"What the hell of it?" Sanlee started to brush past her, but she blocked the door.

"And I distinctly overheard you tell those men that Millie had turned the affairs of Box C over to you, which is a lie and you know it."

He stepped closer, feeling the nape of his neck tighten as he caught the scent of her perfume and saw the swell of her breasts under silk. "You'll have to learn that business is for men. Women can knit an' take care of the kitchen. . . ."

"I am in a business that I manage very well," she shot back at him.

"When we're married . . ." He broke off as he saw the corners of her red mouth begin to tighten. "I gotta get back inside. . . ."

Smiling, he took her arm and steered her to the door that he was opening. But she jerked away.

"What you didn't say, Brad, is that when we're married you intend to take over the store?"

"It's a husband's place, not a wife's. I'll put somebody in there to run it."

She whirled away from him, entered the house and hurried to the stairway.

Sanlee regretted letting it slip about his plans for the store. But it had to come out sooner or later. She'd sulk now, but she'd be over it by the time his guests departed and they could be alone, he assured himself.

It was later when he and the four men were laughing at a joke he had told when he heard a rattle of wheels. From a side window, he saw Isobel heading out, driving a buckboard with a big Diamond Eight branded on its side.

For the rest of the afternoon, the guests at Diamond Eight saw the simmering, volcanic nature of Brad Sanlee. He was polite and would smile with tight lips through his reddish beard, but everyone could tell by the leaden eyes that he was seething.

Buck Rooney decided it was time to pay his respects to the widow Chandler. He hadn't attended Rep's funeral, having been up at Tiempo at the time. In fact, he hadn't even known that the Box C neighbor was dead until he returned home. This time of year there wasn't much to do around his ranch; roundup was over and the cattle had been sold. Now the next big chore was roundup in the fall.

It was an afternoon with a hint of summer's breath that soon would be searing the brush country, drying up creeks and turning the soil to powder. He thought longingly of upstate New York where there were lakes with cooling breezes.

It had been a gamble coming to Texas because he was soon known contemptuously by local residents as a "blue belly." Most of them had fought secession. But he had bought a likely ranch, with money left him by his father, from an old man named Gephart and settled down. At first his New York accent brought frowns, but after a few years, neighbors made a place for him. When he took Sandra, daughter of a Galveston merchant, as his wife, his position was assured. But he had lost both wife and unborn child in the first year of marriage. The brasada was hell on women, so it seemed.

There was another reason for his visit to Box C today. He wanted to have a talk with the foreman. Millie Chandler didn't know how fortunate she was to have a man like Lassiter to take over when her husband died so suddenly. In fact, his neighbor Marcus Kilhaven had said just the other day that it wouldn't surprise him if Lassiter and Rep's widow ended up marrying. Kilhaven's long face was sad as he uttered it, as if such a possibility was almost more than he could bear. Rooney smiled at the memory. Those who knew said that the personable Kilhaven had been crushed when Millie Sanlee had married Rep Chandler.

Rooney knew it would be too far for him to ride all the way home that day, so he'd spend the night at the Box C bunkhouse, as was customary.

He was following a trail through the brush that would soon lead him to wheel tracks, the Box C road, when he heard a rattle of gunfire dead ahead. . . .

19

From time to time after leaving Santos, Lassiter would look over his shoulder to see if he could spot any threatening riders. He was as sure that the Texas sun burned down on the back of his neck as he was that Hobart had gotten word to Sanlee about the money. At the bank, when he had turned the money back in, it had shown on Hobart's face—mostly in his eyes.

Well, he'd soon be home and to hell with any possible threat this day from Sanlee. He urged the team to a faster pace. It was the rattle of the hack wagon wheels and the pounding of hooves from the team that drowned out sounds of approaching horsemen.

But at last, where the road struck a long stretch of sand and the sounds of the wagon and team were diminished, he heard them coming. As sharp as a sudden clap of thunder on a still day was the ominous rush of hoofbeats.

Looking back, he saw them, three riders charging diagonally along a game trail through the brush, avoiding overhanging mesquite branches. Their hat brims were turned up from pressure of wind against their faces. He recognized them instantly—Doane because of his enormous size, burly Joe Tige and Pinto George with the whitish hair and pale eyes. Each of them bent low in the saddle of speeding mounts.

With his wagon moving at a good clip, Lassiter transferred the reins to his left hand and leaned down to pick up his rifle from the floorboards. Putting the rifle stock between his knees like a vise, he worked the loading lever with his right hand. He was about to fire single-handedly as if it were a pistol when two things happened simultaneously.

The road made a sudden sharp bend. And the whirling right front wheel hit a deep soft spot. Lassiter felt the speeding wagon tilt. With a chill in his gut, he was flung out as if fired from a cannon. For an instant he had an upside-down view of the sky, then of earth. He let his rifle go in midair. Although deep sand broke his fall, he still struck with enough force to daze him and jar breath from his body. Just as he came down he had enough presence of mind to clamp his right hand to his holstered gun. Holding it in place as he rolled, he barely managed to escape the overturning wagon. The wagon tongue was wrenched loose in the spill. He had a distorted view of the team running madly up the road. A great cloud of dust and sand shot into the sky from the tongue they were dragging.

Two of the riders started to fire at him, but Doane bellowed, "I want him *alive!*"

It was Joe Tige who was nearest, mounted on a red roan. Firing at a gallop threw off his aim. It did the same for Pinto George. Geysers of sand stung Lassiter's cheek. A reminder of an evening when bullets into a dirt floor had temporarily blinded him.

He threw up his forearm to shield his eyes from the sand. Then he rolled aside as the red roan was leaping toward him. He fired, the bullet plowing into the roan's neck and on into Tige's chest. As the roan flashed past, blood pumping from the neck wound, it stumbled and went down head first. Tige was thrown like a bundle of rags.

Momentum had carried Doane and Pinto George some distance beyond the overturned wagon. Now they were reining in. Sand spurted as they turned their horses. Doane had a big knife clamped in his teeth, giving notice of what he intended to do with it. A gleaming .45 was gripped in his oversized hand.

Lassiter sprang for the wagon, which rested on its side, one splintered wheel still turning slowly. He fired twice but Pinto George was reining toward some mesquite. The shot missed. And as he drew a bead on the man for another try, there was a flurry of hoofbeats from the east. Buck Rooney appeared suddenly in the road. Because he was directly behind George and Doane, Lassiter was forced to hold his fire. He yelled at Rooney to get away.

Rooney could not quite comprehend the scene thrust upon him so suddenly. He pulled up and then started a belated try for his holstered revolver. But Doane rammed in the spurs. With a squeal of pain, his big Morgan lunged. It put Doane close enough so that one huge arm swept Rooney out of the saddle and dumped him in the sand. At that moment, Pinto George resumed firing. Bullets crashed through the underside of the wagon where Lassiter had taken refuge. Mingled with waves of dust was a layer of blue-black gunsmoke.

"Rooney . . . duck!" Lassiter shouted at him. He was afraid to fire at Doane and perhaps risk putting a bullet in Rooney. But in the next second or so, Doane was out of the saddle. He landed behind Rooney, who was dazed but sitting up.

"Hold it, George!" Doane yelled, allowing only a wedge of his face to project beyond Rooney's heavy shoulder. "Lassiter, throw down your gun, or I'll kill Rooney. Hear me, I'll *kill him!*"

Rooney cried out in pain as Doane rammed the barrel of his gun into the rancher's ear and twisted it.

In that moment, Lassiter saw Pinto George, twenty feet away, grinning from the saddle of a sweated sorrel. A wisp of blue smoke trailed from the barrel of his revolver. Tige, on the ground nearby, had moved his arm and was trying to sit up. A stain across the front of his gray wool shirt had widened. His head hung loosely and he seemed to be in pain. Behind Rooney, Doane was huddled, the knife no longer clamped between his large teeth but stuck in the sand. What could be seen of the blade glittered in the sunlight. He drew Rooney's gun and threw it over his shoulder into the brush.

As Lassiter looked on, he saw Doane's big thumb cock the gun held at Rooney's ear. Rooney's face was slack and in his eyes was an awareness of imminent death.

"Let Rooney go," Lassiter called, knowing he had no choice.

"Rooney rides out, but you stay!" Doane shouted. "Drop that gun!"

Unless he wanted Rooney's blood on his hands, Lassiter knew he had to obey. Slowly, he got to his feet and let his gun drop.

"Turn him loose," Lassiter said, holding his two

hands shoulder high so Doane could see that he was up to no tricks.

Satisfied, Doane hauled Rooney to his feet and walked him to the wagon that was tipped on its side. His small eyes searched the ground. "Where the hell's the money?" he yelled suddenly.

"I turned it back to the bank," Lassiter said. "It looks like Hobart didn't get word to Sanlee in time to let him know the change in plans." He was stalling for time because Rooney was now blinking his eyes, taking deep breaths as he recovered his senses. He had been dazed since Doane's long arm had swept him out of the saddle.

Doane kept twisting, grinding the barrel of the .45 into Rooney's ear, making the man grimace with pain.

"Leave him alone," Lassiter said in a dead voice. "I've told you how it'll be."

"It'll be you dead . . . slowly." Scars danced on Doane's face as he broke into a wide grin. "You cost us too damn much to let you off easy."

Rooney stiffened his shoulders and cranked his head around to look back at Doane. "You'll never get away with killin' him," Rooney said in a voice trying desperately to be firm.

Doane gave him a rude shove while keeping his eyes on Lassiter beside the upturned wagon. Pinto George was searching the edges of the clearing for the money.

"Ain't a sign of it, Shorty," he said finally with a shake of his head. His bony frame with its minimum padding of flesh was covered with a striped shirt and canvas pants. His boots were worn, as was the stained sombrero tipped back from a fringe of whitish hair. The next thing Lassiter knew, George was ramming a gun against his back.

"What'd you do with the money?" George demanded.

"I told you," Lassiter snarled, not looking around.

"Likely he seen us comin' an' throwed it out," Doane said. "Go back a ways an' have a look."

"An' leave you here with the two of 'em?" George shook his head. "I'll bust Lassiter over the head, then go have a look."

But Doane said, "Hold it, Pinto. I want Lassiter able to talk, at least for a while."

"Yeah," George agreed. "The easy way is to make Lassiter talk about the money."

Doane gave Rooney another shove. The rancher took a few stumbling steps toward Lassiter.

"Don't forget our agreement, Doane," Lassiter reminded heavily. "Rooney goes free."

Doane failed to reply. He holstered his gun and plucked the knife he had returned to his boot top. "Keep a gun on him, Pinto."

Gripping the knife, Doane came plodding toward Lassiter, brushing past Rooney, who looked on fearfully. "I ask you once again about the money," Doane said ominously as he halted in front of Lassiter.

"And I told you. . . ."

Quick as a striking snake, the knife flashed out. The blade, glittering in the sunlight, flicked across Lassiter's throat—not a deep cut, just through the skin. Blood ran down Lassiter's neck and into his shirt. But his cold blue eyes never wavered.

"Let Rooney ride away," Lassiter said again.

But he could see that Doane had no intention of honoring their agreement. Lassiter braced himself as Doane, baring large, yellow teeth, lifted his right arm slightly so that a wine-colored stain on the blade could clearly be seen. Doane held the weapon like a swordsman, which announced that he was an experienced knife fighter.

Pinto George had eased off the pressure of the gun against Lassiter's backbone but was still behind him. Lassiter felt cold sweat dampen his armpits but no fear showed on his face. One thing was for sure, he had no intention of standing still and allowing Doane to cut him a second time, which he was intending to do. Lassiter could read it in his narrowed eyes. It would be better to have his spine shattered by a bullet than to go out like a stuck hog, bleeding his life away into the sandy Texas soil.

One moment was all it took for this to pass through his mind. And then he was doubling up, hurling himself at Doane's knees. He felt the massive forearm brush across his shoulder blades, the knife came that close to cutting him again. Then the two of them were tumbling across the ground. The blade of the stained knife flashed like a diamond in the sun when it was jarred from Doane's hand.

Tension threw a barb of pain across the back of Lassiter's neck as he braced for the slam of bullets from George's gun. The man's gun did explode, but not at Lassiter. Rooney had taken the opportunity when Lassiter and Doane were on the ground to leap and try to seize George's gun. The force of two bullets in Buck Rooney's chest hurled him against a mesquite. As he toppled to the ground, Lassiter was throwing himself behind the wrecked wagon. His outstretched hands broke his fall, but he came down as intended, near the rifle he had dropped in the sand. Although it might be fouled with sand and explode in his face, he had to take that chance.

Doane, who had been knocked flat on his back, was just picking himself up. Pinto George raced around behind the upended wagon, his pale eyes reflecting rage at Lassiter's trickery.

Lassiter threw himself to one side, but knew he was too late. He felt a jarring shock in his left shoulder as George fired. But he managed to lift his rifle. He heard a gritty sound of sand on metal when he touched the trigger. Nothing happened. Although he knew the weapon was fouled with sand, he tried again. Still nothing. It was then that he became aware of George yelling something to Doane about riders coming. Then Lassiter was aware of a drumroll of hoofbeats from the direction of Box C. Riders were coming at a dead run.

Intent only on saving their own necks now, Doane and George leaped into the saddle. Doane was swearing at George, who answered, "Hell, you told me you wanted Lassiter *alive!*"

"Not now I don't." And as Doane flashed by the spot where Lassiter had last been seen behind the wagon, he fired three quick shots. But Lassiter had withdrawn into a mesquite thicket. He heard the bullets make thunking sounds into wood.

Hardly had George and Doane disappeared at the bend in the road before Luis Herrera and five Box C riders were drawing rein in a great cloud of dust.

"We heard shots!" Herrera shouted when Lassiter stumbled from the brush where he had taken refuge. "We came as fast as we could."

The eyes of Herrera and of his riders widened when they saw the thin cut across Lassiter's throat, the blood-soaked shirt, and a soggy wetness at the top of the left shoulder.

Lassiter looked at the spot where he had last seen Joe Tige lying on the ground. But sometime in the interim the wounded man had somehow managed to stagger to his horse and ride away, unnoticed.

Some of the men were already looking at Rooney, who lay crumpled beyond the wagon. Lassiter stumbled over and knelt beside Rooney. The man was still alive, but barely. His face and lips were bloodless and his eyes reflected pain and shock. Although Lassiter felt light in the head from the loss of blood, he managed to give Herrera a brief account of what had happened.

"We'll go after 'em," Herrera said with an oath and turned for his horse.

But Lassiter shook his head. "Let 'em go. For now."

Then he was giving orders. Somebody was to catch Rooney's horse, which had wandered off down the road.

Rooney's eyes were open and there was even a faint smile on his pale lips. "You jumpin' Doane saved our bacon," he said in a voice so low that Lassiter had to bend down to hear him. Lassiter smiled encouragement but wondered just how much good he had done for Rooney by the bold move.

It was evident that the rancher was in bad shape and might not even last the two miles to Box C. He didn't. After half a mile, he nearly toppled from the saddle. Lassiter—riding on one side, Herrera on the other—saved him from the fall. But a quick examination showed there was no pulse. Rooney was dead.

An enraged Lassiter helped tie the body over the back of the horse. Death of the neighbor at the hands of Diamond Eight men was almost too much.

At the ranch, he cut around in back of the barn, hoping to avoid Millie until he could get cleaned up. But she happened to be in the yard and saw his shirt stained a deep red. A fist flew to her mouth. Then she stiffened in shock as she saw the body roped to the back of a sorrel.

"Somebody's dead," she said in hushed tones. "Who is it?"

"Rooney," Lassiter answered.

"Oh, my God."

Herrera had given Lassiter a hand down from the saddle. As soon as he stood shakily on solid ground, Millie, unmindful of the bloodied shirt, flung an arm around Lassiter's waist.

"You're coming to the house," she announced firmly, "where I can take care of you."

By then he was so tired, in such low spirits because of what had happened to Rooney, that he didn't argue with her. While she tried to put him into one of the spare bedrooms, he chose instead the big sofa in the parlor. He sank down and stared blankly at the big stone fireplace. Millie had hurried to the kitchen to heat water, her pretty face taut with strain.

Soon she had his shirt off, his long johns pulled to the waist and was sponging off the blood. Although the wound at his throat was superficial, she cringed when mentioning that a little more pressure on the knife and Lassiter would have been dead.

What had caused the most blood loss was a gash at the top of the left shoulder where a bullet cut through the flesh. Fortunately, the slug had not lodged in the wound but continued on its way.

As she applied bandages to the wounds, she asked him to tell her in detail just what had happened. When he finished relating the attack in the brush, he said, "My fault, damn it. Your brother got wind that I was goin' to carry money home. But what he didn't know was that I'd changed my mind. I had a strong hunch something like that might happen."

"You only did what you thought was right."

"When you came home and told me Hobart wouldn't honor the bank draft, I wanted to shove it down his throat."

"I can understand that. . . ."

"But I went too far in taking the money."

"But what else could you do, Lassiter? He refused to accept the bank draft."

"Well, he's honoring it now, which I should've made him do in the first place."

"Don't blame yourself."

"But I do. If Doane and the others hadn't been after the money they thought I had, Rooney would still be alive."

She sank back on her heels, looking grim. "I repeat, it wasn't your fault, Lassiter. Not at all." Then she picked up a pan of pinkish water and carried it out the back door.

His first chore was to clean his weapons. The rifle had malfunctioned, having been fouled with sand. He couldn't afford to let it happen again. He had to be ready for the showdown that had been postponed much too long.

Millie returned after a few minutes, carrying one of his clean shirts and his razor. "You're going to stay in this house where I can keep an eye on you."

He shook his head. "What would the men think?" he asked with a wry smile.

"I don't give one damn what they think." Her lips trembled and she seemed close to tears. She reached for Lassiter's hand and gave it a squeeze. But he did not respond. He was thinking of what they had to face. Word would have to be sent to Sheriff Doak Palmer up at Tiempo about Rooney's death instead of reporting it to a local deputy. The long-time deputy in Santos had died six months before and the sheriff had not gotten around to appointing a replacement—due to Diamond Eight, some hinted. Sanlee wanted more or less of a free hand until he had his cattle empire intact.

There was also Rooney's funeral to face.

"Does Rooney have any relatives?" he asked Millie.

She said she didn't think so. "At least none of them ever came for his wife's funeral. Frankly, I think he was alone in the world. And now he's gone, poor man."

When he started to dismantle his weapons for cleaning, his hands shook so much that he had to give it up for the present. But he did brace himself for the task of writing to Sheriff Palmer, explaining the death of Rooney, naming the man responsible, Pinto George. Lassiter always suspected the name was an alias. His handwriting was shaky and when he had finished there were numerous ink blots. He started a letter to the undertaker but had to give up. Millie finished it for him.

One of the men would be sent to Santos with the two letters. The one to the sheriff would go north on the morning stage.

He was on the mend and soon he would be ready for any eventuality. . . .

20

Lassiter's insistence to sleep on the sofa, he knew all too well, was only a futile attempt to postpone the inevitable. When it did happen, finally, the act between him and Millie was as natural as breathing. They had finished supper and he insisted on shaving thin slices of yellow lye soap into a pan to do the dishes.

"You're a remarkable man," she said solemnly, watching him from a kitchen chair. "Tough as cold steel in one way, yet gentle in another."

"Not many would agree on the latter," he said with a short laugh.

When the dishes were done and she had given him a towel to dry his hands, their eyes met. He dropped the towel and impulsively reached for her. And she responded, her arms warm against the back of his neck. He picked her up and carried her to the rear of the big house. He forgot about the healing shoulder.

"Not in there," she said softly when he approached the bedroom she had shared with Rep Chandler.

"I didn't figure to," he said and, in a back bedroom, lowered her gently to a bed. Moonlight filtered through lacy white curtains and turned the room to pale yellow. There was a headboard of polished dark wood. A strip of Mexican rug put color in the room. A night table beside the bed held a lamp with a rose-colored shade.

After a time of heady exploration, they came together, their eager bodies struggling in an ancient ritual. Occasionally, her muted cries of pleasure broke the stillness of the lonely house. Tree branches gently scraped across roof tiles as a breeze came up.

The only time he froze was when her arms locked across his broad back and she cried out, "Now I've got you, got you *forever!*"

Then she collapsed. For several minutes while he held her close, she did not open her eyes. When she did, it was to smile happily up into his shadowed face.

When the funeral for Buck Rooney was finally held, it was not well attended. Business establishments in Santos closed for the ceremony. Isobel Hartney in a new dress, her favorite color of green, was there with parasol over a shoulder.

"I don't believe in morbidity," she explained when one of the women mentioned that she wasn't wearing black.

Isobel smiled. Her busy eyes searched the sparse crowd and settled on Lassiter, who was late in arriving. Clinging to his arm was Millie Chandler, her dark hair shining in the sun. Isobel realized she suddenly hated her.

A solemn Brad Sanlee rode in from his ranch. For

once he was alone. He seemed unusually reserved, most everyone thought, and decided he apparently was deeply affected by Buck Rooney's death. No one had realized they were that close, a man near Lassiter was explaining to a neighbor. Lassiter smiled grimly.

Marcus Kilhaven spoke gravely to Millie and shook hands with Lassiter. He mentioned his late friend, Rooney, in his usual quiet way. A black suit, obviously purchased some years before, did not quite fit his tall, raw-boned frame.

This time a traveling reverend happened to be on hand, so the ceremony was lengthy, not abbreviated as had been the case with Rep Chandler.

Tate, Kilhaven's nearest neighbor with the exception of the deceased Buck Rooney, was not present. When someone whispered a question, it was revealed that Tate had sold out to Brad Sanlee, suddenly, and left that part of Texas. Upon overhearing this low-voiced exchange, Lassiter couldn't help but be reminded of the list Sanlee had shoved under his nose at their initial meeting that day in O'Leary's Saloon. Kilhaven, Tate and Rooney. Now only Kilhaven remained.

All during the ceremony, Sanlee avoided Lassiter's eyes. The reverend was extolling the earthly virtues of the late Buck Rooney, whom he had never met.

When Brad Sanlee was riding out, Millie stared at his broad back and whispered, "He's up to something. I know him so well."

Lassiter was also staring at Sanlee, a look of cold blue winter in his eyes.

"Suddenly, I'm afraid," Millie said shakily. She clung to Lassiter's arm as if it were an anchor to keep her from slipping off the face of the spinning earth.

The funeral had purposely been delayed so as to

give the sheriff time to come down from Tiempo. But he hadn't come. Nor had there been any word from him regarding the letter Lassiter had sent.

After the funeral, Millie found herself encircled by women firing questions. How was she getting along since the death of her husband? Some of them cast sly glances at the tall, dark Lassiter standing nearby. Isobel came gliding up with a rustle of her stylish dress.

"You see, I was right," she said softly with a tight smile. "You didn't like it when I pointed out a fact to you one day."

"What fact?" he snapped and instantly regretted it.

"A charming widow and a ranch . . ."

Lassiter's attention was drawn to Arthur Hobart, who stood a few feet away. There was a secret smile on the banker's smooth, round face. When he found Lassiter watching him, he averted his gaze but did not lose the smile. Seeing it caused a chill to slide down Lassiter's backbone. He thoughtfully fingered the clean white bandage Millie had placed around his throat that morning. Something deep within warned him to get out before he brought disaster to Rep's widow. He had lingered much too long in this Texas brush country.

On the way back to Box C, Luis Herrera and three of the vaqueros trailed the buckboard. Lassiter was driving. The subject of his leaving Texas came up. But each time Millie interrupted with her bright and eager voice, pointing out exceptionally colorful huisache blossoms or pointing at the sky where giant clouds were whipped into gargantuan shapes by the wind.

"They look like castles," she exclaimed. "Can't you see castles up there, Lassiter?"

"Millie, listen to me. . . ."

"I think the tribute to Mr. Rooney was sweet but much too long. When my time comes, which I'm sure will be years away, I hope we'll be buried together in the ranch plot. I'm sure Rep wouldn't mind."

Lassiter felt a dull pain that wasn't altogether from his healing wounds.

The trouble came with the suddenness of a spring storm where the sky is the bluest of blue one minute, then spouting rain and violent wind a quarter of an hour later. He had gone into Santos to confront Arthur Hobart at his bank. He was remembering the banker's sly smile the day of Rooney's funeral.

"I want you to show me in your books where you credited the $37,000 dollars to the Chandler account."

Now that Hobart was alone with Lassiter, with not even the gaunt clerk nearby, he was not so cocky. With trembling hands, he got out a ledger, flipped pages and then pointed to an entry.

Lassiter nodded. "Just figured to make sure."

"Anything I can ever do for you, Lassiter, just say the word."

Lassiter looked at the round face, the mound of belly and the nervous hands. Why was Hobart so obsequious all of a sudden? he asked himself. Was it fear? Or was it knowledge that coming events would set things right in his favor?

"I'll be leaving here," Lassiter said coldly. "And I expect you to treat Millie Chandler decently."

"As you've been treating her, I expect," Hobart said with a straight face.

"What'd you mean by that?"

Hobart paled. "I . . . I . . . it just slipped out. I meant nothing."

"I know what you meant." Lassiter gave him a look that caused the banker's jaw to drop. "Watch your talk, Hobart. Or I'll find some way to wash the dirt out of your mind with lye soap."

As he rode along the alley behind the bank, he saw from a corner of his eye Isobel Hartney dash from the rear of her store and wave to him. She was wearing a large apron, the inevitable pencil under the yellow hair at her ear. When he ignored the wave, she called to him. But he rode on, his face tight. In his present mood he didn't trust her any farther than he could throw an ox.

He set his horse to a canter. By the time he arrived back at Box C, the animal was lathered and Lassiter's clothing sticky with perspiration. It was an overcast day that kept the growing heat pressed to the ground as if with a giant tent. There seemed to be no one around the corral or bunkhouse. He thought it strange. Usually there was at least one man at the home place. Cottonwood branches seemed to droop in the heat.

Esperanza Herrera had just washed her hair and was drying it on the porch of the small house she shared with her husband. He rode over and asked about her husband and the crew. Where were they? She threw back the long damp hair over a shoulder and looked up at him in the saddle of his lathered horse. "Luis say you give orders."

"Orders for what?"

"To take the whole crew and go over east to move cattle away from Kilhaven's boundary. To clear out that end of the range."

"I said that?" Well, to tell the truth, he had been thinking it. With Tate having sold out and Rooney dead, Sanlee's next move would logically be against

Kilhaven, one way or another. Perhaps he had mentioned it to Herrera. He couldn't rightly remember. But he was a little miffed that Herrera had taken it upon himself to do the job without talking it over first.

"I don't understand why Luis thought I ordered him to do it."

"It was Señor Barkley who bring word."

"Barkley?" He was the new man Herrera had hired on to replace one of the vaqueros who had quit after Rep Chandler's funeral. Lassiter stared down at the woman. "What's Barkley got to do with it?"

"He come an' he say he run into you on the way to town. An' you give orders for Luis to take the whole crew an' go over to Kilhaven's line."

"The whole crew, eh?" Lassiter stiffened in the saddle, his blue eyes sweeping the ranch yard. He looked at the big house in the cottonwoods some distance away. "Is Mrs. Chandler home?"

"I do not know for sure, señor." The woman explained that she had been out back washing the family clothes and then her hair.

"How long ago did Luis and the men leave?"

"Right after you go to town." Her brown face showed concern. "Is something wrong?"

"I dunno. Maybe." The whole damn thing didn't add up. Barkley telling Luis Herrera that he, Lassiter, had issued orders to move cattle away from Kilhaven's line. And to take the whole crew. It smelled worse than a dead skunk in July heat. He turned his horse and started for the house.

21

Earlier that morning, Isobel Hartney and her two clerks were using feather dusters in the store. Her blond hair was pinned up, making her look quite regal despite a voluminous apron with its straps across her slender back. She had been dusting a windowsill when she happened to look out to see Brad Sanlee enter town with some of his men. They dismounted in front of O'Leary's. The men went inside and Brad came walking toward the store.

She could tell by Brad's tense face that something was up. Usually she didn't open the store this early, but it was Saturday and yesterday had been the first of the month, payday on the ranches, a double reason for being ready for business.

At first she thought of having her clerks tell Brad that she was indisposed. She hadn't seen him since the day she had abruptly left his guests and driven herself home in one of his wagons. But she had to face him sometime. Why not today?

A scowling Brad jerked open the side door, letting

it slam back against its stop. "I figured you'd still be in bed," he said in a nasty voice. The two clerks lost the color in their faces. When Sanlee was in one of his moods, there was no telling just what the next few minutes might hold.

He swaggered over to her, big and bearded, a gun swinging at his hip. He got her by an arm and hurried her at a stumbling run to the foot of the rear stairs where they would be out of earshot of the clerks.

"You ran out on me the other day," he accused, leaning close so she had the full impact of his glittering gray eyes. But she didn't flinch.

"I'd had enough of you for one day." Her chin lifted.

He grinned. "I just thought you'd like to know about Buck Rooney."

"What about him?" Something made her heart lurch.

"Lassiter murdered him."

"Come now, Brad, that's preposterous and you know it." But her mouth was dry and her eyes enormous.

"We got a witness."

She tried to slow her pounding heart. "What witness?"

"Doc Clayburn."

"You're making this up to . . . to frighten me."

"Doc had been worryin' about my sis losin' her husband. He was on his way out to Box C to find out if she might be needin' a tonic or somethin'."

"Do you mean to tell me that Doc witnessed Lassiter murder Buck Rooney?" She sounded incredulous.

"He was right there in the brush. Rooney an' Lassiter wasn't more'n twenty feet away. He could see an' hear most everything. Lassiter didn't like somethin' Rooney said to him, so Doc says. Doc was too far away to really know what Rooney said. But he sure seen Lassiter whip out a gun an' kill him."

"You're making this up to frighten me." She was clasping her hands at her breasts so tightly that her knuckles were white as bleached bone. The sounds of her two clerks arranging merchandise in the store were faint. Her heart pounded.

"Doc's ready to swear in court," Sanlee said triumphantly.

"Somebody should get word to Sheriff Palmer."

"He's already got word from me."

The shaft of cold fear that had pierced her heart was now shifting to anger. "You and the sheriff," she said, her red lips barely moving. "Yes, I begin to see it all now."

"Once Lassiter's done for, maybe I'll come around to see how you feel about marryin' up with me. But then again, maybe I won't."

"Brad, if you do something to Lassiter it will *really* be murder. The law will . . ."

"Hell, honey, I *am* the law." Grinning broadly, he pulled out a badge. He showed it to her. She wasn't surprised. The sheriff and Brad's late father had been close. At election time, the elder Sanlee had made sure that most voters chose Doak Palmer to remain in office. And Brad had taken over from his father.

"So you see, if I should happen to arrest Lassiter an' he makes a break for it . . . well, I got no choice but to bring him in."

"With a shot in the back," she flung at him bitterly.

"I'll yell myself hoarse tellin' him to halt. But finally I'll have no choice but to get him. 'Course I'll aim for a leg, but you know how things go when a fella is runnin' full tilt, tryin' to get away. A bullet don't always go where you aim."

"Brad, you are a rotten son of a bitch!" Tears of rage and fear spilled from her large eyes.

Instead of anger at what she had said, he threw back his head and bellowed with laughter. At the door he said, "I'll be back, so get yourself prettied up. Reckon I'll be marryin' with you after all."

Wiping her eyes, she ran after him, realizing all of a sudden that reviling him would not help Lassiter in the least. She tugged at his shirt sleeve. "Brad, let's have coffee and talk about this."

"Talk about what?"

"I just can't believe that Doc Clayburn . . ."

"Believe it." Grinning, he pulled her fingers from his shirt and started over to O'Leary's. She saw him enter the saloon. When he didn't emerge immediately with his men, she breathed a little easier.

Isobel poured water from a pitcher into a basin and washed her eyes, dried her face on a towel, then told her clerks she had some business to attend to. She hurried out into the clear morning and walked rapidly toward the building where Doc Clayburn had his office and living quarters. It was a narrow, two-story building that stood alone at the eastern edge of town. It was surrounded by a great tangle of mesquite and cottonwoods intended to help mask the activities of the former residents. When Isobel was a young girl, it had been a brothel. Being naturally curious, she used to walk home from school to pass the building. She would stand across the street in the trees and note who came and went. She became such a fixture that some of the girls would at times laugh and wave to her from the windows. Finally her father got wind of what she was doing and campaigned to have the place closed down. Due to his efforts, such activities were now carried on at a place called Big Creek, three miles out of town. It was not a creek at all, but a very dry wash.

After much knocking and calling his name, Isobel finally got Doc Clayburn to come to his office door. He was bleary-eyed and reeked of alcohol. "Miss Hartney," he said with so deep a bow that he nearly lost his balance. "What brings you here so early in the morning?"

"Doc, Brad Sanlee just told me that you witnessed Lassiter murder Buck Rooney." She saw his face tighten. He straightened his shoulders.

She shoved her way into the narrow, cluttered room and closed the door at her back. There was a chemical smell from bottles on a long table. There was a pestle and mortar with a grayish substance in the bottom. Some of it had spilled onto the table. There was also a quart bottle of whiskey with only an inch of dark brown liquid left in it. Next to it was a dirty glass. This morning Doc Clayburn seemed to have aged since the last time she had seen him, which was only a few days before. His rather large sideburns only accentuated his thin and haggard face.

"You . . . you'll have to excuse me, Miss Hartney. I'm expecting a patient."

"Didn't you hear what I said?" she demanded, leaning down to his height.

It seemed as if the strength had suddenly gone out of his legs. He sank to a padded leather chair, pale and grim. Finally, after much prodding from her, he began to talk. He spoke of a time when he was much younger, back in the state of New York.

"My wife took a fancy to a neighbor. I killed him. Then I turned the gun on my terrified wife, but I couldn't pull the trigger. Because she was the mother of our baby daughter. The man I found in my wife's embrace had friends and influence. Had I stayed, I would have been executed. My daughter is now a mother with children of her own. My arrest would be devastating to her." He lifted his hands and let them plop to his knees.

"And now Brad's told you to lie about Lassiter or he'll see you arrested."

"One day I foolishly mentioned the New York killing to Brad. He was only a boy then, but he never forgot. I'd had too much whiskey that day and I was despondent because I'd just received a letter from my daughter. Even after all that had happened, we still corresponded. She wrote that my wife, her mother, had died. As a result, I was in a melancholy mood that day and needed someone to talk to. . . ."

"You can't just accuse Lassiter."

"For myself, I don't care," he said wearily. "But my daughter, my only child. Disgrace would be shattering and Brad let me know that he would get word to the law in New York."

"You'd accuse an innocent man?"

"Isobel, face facts. Lassiter is a known killer." She started to interrupt, but he waved her to silence. "He's gone unpunished for God knows how many crimes. So in a way it's justice."

"Not justice but cowardice on your part. Face up to Brad. Defy him. It's only his word against yours about that business back in New York."

He gave her a sad smile and said, "Then you don't know Brad very well."

"Oh, I know him."

"Yes," he said after a moment of searching her eyes, "I guess you do."

She felt herself flush. But this morning there was more at stake than her indiscretions. It was a man's life. At first she tried to reason with him, but he kept shaking his head. Finally she lost her temper. He got up from the chair, squared his shoulders and asked her to leave.

"What's a worthless life like Lassiter's?" he demanded when she hesitated. "His life weighed against the well-being of my daughter and grandchildren?"

"Lassiter's isn't a worthless life," she said stiffly. "He's honorable and decent. It's men like Brad who've spread those vile stories about him."

"Ah, women," he said, peering at her out of bloodshot eyes, "always entranced by a rogue."

"Doc. I'm ashamed at you."

"Perhaps. But remember this. As you reminded me that it was only Brad's word against mine, so it's the same between you and me. If you reveal this discussion we've had this morning, I'll deny it." He looked resolute and for the first time his gaze was unwavering.

Troubled by what she had learned, she wondered what to do. Perhaps Lassiter would be in town today, since it was Saturday. Or at least some of his men would be in. She could send a message that she had to see him. On the way back to her store, she walked near enough to O'Leary's hitching post to see that the Diamond Eight horses were still there. At least Brad wasn't making an immediate move.

It was over two hours later that she happened to see Lassiter riding along the alley from the direction of the bank. Rushing to the rear door, she waved and called to him, but he ignored her and rode rapidly away. At first she was so angered by his rudeness that she almost hated him. Then later she calmed down and thought seriously about the danger he faced.

There was one thing she didn't realize. Over an hour before, Brad and his men had left O'Leary's, riding west out of town so they wouldn't have to pass her store.

22

Esperanza Herrera had gone back into her small house and closed the door. Lassiter was riding toward the headquarters of Box C, the big adobe in the cluster of cottonwoods. He had just dismounted in front of the house, hurrying up the veranda steps, when his ears picked up the distinctive clack of a shod hoof on rock. His head jerked around in the direction of the sound. He froze at the sight of men riding up through the cottonwoods by the barn.

Spinning around, he started running back down the veranda steps, intending to grab his rifle from the saddle boot. But he had only taken two steps when he heard a squeak of hinges as the door at his back was suddenly opened.

"Hold it, Lassiter!" It was Brad Sanlee's amused voice.

Lassiter looked over his shoulder. One of Sanlee's arms was tight around Millie's slender waist, his fingers gripping a .45 aimed at Lassiter. The other hand was across his half-sister's mouth. Her eyes were wild with mingled fury and alarm. She tried to struggle there in the doorway of the big house, but Sanlee was too strong.

As Lassiter stood frozen on the veranda step, Doane and Pinto George came riding around one corner of the house. From the opposite direction appeared Joe Tige, the upper edge of a dirty bandage at the open collar of his shirt. At his side was Jeddy Quine with the drooping left eyelid, and the new Box C hand, Pete Barkley, the turncoat. As they rode up through the cottonwoods by the barn, there was a smug look on Barkley's face. He chewed tobacco and spat a brown stream.

"Stand hitched, Lassiter," came Sanlee's voice at his back. "Don't even twitch a finger. You'll do that if you think anything at all of my kid sister. If not, well . . ." He let it hang there with all the ugly connotations.

Lassiter clenched his teeth. Everything flashed across Lassiter's mind like a streak of lightning: to come all this way, fight all the battles and have it end like this. And just as quickly it was gone. He straightened his shoulders and spoke firmly.

"Leave your sister out of it. This is between you an' me."

"Yeah, it sure is, Lassiter." Sanlee chuckled. "You got that part of it right, anyhow. Now you back up the steps. Slow an' easy. An' don't look around. I'll tell you when to stop."

Lassiter eyed the men who were watching him with tight amusement from their saddles—all except Joe Tige, whom he had shot the day Rooney died. Tige glared.

Knowing he had no choice, under the circumstances, Lassiter backed slowly until Sanlee called a halt. He felt a gun rammed against his spine. Although he did not look around, he could hear the strangled sounds of anger made by Millie against the hand pressed over her mouth.

At Sanlee's order, Pinto George dismounted and ran lightly up the veranda steps. The pale eyes were mocking as he gingerly reached out and unbuckled Lassiter's gun belt. Then he stepped back, wrapped the belt around the holstered revolver and threw it over the railing into some geraniums that Millie had been trying to grow.

"With your fangs pulled, you're kinda harmless-lookin'," Sanlee said jovially. He had removed his hand from Millie's mouth. She turned on him in rage, but he only laughed.

Then she said to Lassiter, "He came sneaking in the back door before I knew what happened." She seemed close to tears of anger and frustration. "Now he's got some crazy idea. . . ."

"I told her she's gonna marry Marcus Kilhaven," Sanlee said bluntly. "An' she is."

"No!" she cried. "It worked once with Rep Chandler, but not again!"

"It'll work again, sis."

"Damn you, Brad, you can't force me. . . ."

"I can an' I will." His voice hardened. "You know how things are done around here."

"Don't bother to tell me."

"You're a widow lady an' I'm your brother. An' I step in an' take over. An' I say what's best for you. You marryin' Kilhaven is best."

"Best for you, you mean!" she screamed and tried to claw his face. But he gripped her two wrists in one large hand. His smile was ugly through the beard. "Spitfire, that's what you are. I reckon Kilhaven will sure appreciate that in a wife."

When she tried to run, Sanlee grabbed her shoulder and spun her around. Her hair swung wildly and the shoulder of her dress ripped down to the top of a white camisole. A nipple and the upper part of a breast showed through the thin material.

"Keep an eye on Lassiter!" Sanlee shouted angrily at the ring of staring riders around the veranda. Five of them Lassiter remembered from roundup, but he didn't know their names. But they had the mark of toughness in lean faces as did the others.

Then Sanlee pulled Millie back into the house and threw a coat over her shoulders. He pushed her back to the porch.

"Two of you hitch up a wagon an' be quick about it!" Sanlee ordered. Two of the men hurried to the corral.

Never had Lassiter felt so completely helpless. If he turned and tried to give Millie a hand, he'd likely take a bullet in the spine. And at the same time his very move could endanger Millie. During the interval while a team was being hitched to one of the buckboards, Lassiter stood stiffly, his back to Sanlee. He was trying to calmly talk Sanlee into letting Millie go and settle the score between the two of them, man to man.

"You claim you saw me stand up to Doc Kelmmer that time in Tucson," Lassiter reminded. "Let's you and me go at it the same."

"You been takin' laudanum for those wounds of yours, it seems like. An' it's made your head soft. I don't aim to stand up to you. I aim to beat you to your knees. We oughta have a velvet collar for you, Lassiter. 'Cause the hang rope might tear open that cut on your throat. That'd be a shame now, wouldn't it?"

All of the men laughed and some slapped themselves on their thighs with glee.

Millie's face went dead white as she stared up into her half-brother's face. "You didn't mean what you said . . . surely you didn't. . . ."

"I aim to hang him."

Millie screamed.

At Sanlee's order, Doane came up and seized Lassiter from behind and lifted him off his feet. It made Lassiter feel like a small boy being embraced by a madman. He lashed out with his feet all the way down the steps. But with one of Doane's thick arms around his waist, the other pinning his chest, he was helpless.

Doane's breath smelled of stale whiskey and tobacco. "I aim to finish what I started with the knife," Doane said softly through his teeth.

Then Doane swung Lassiter up and sat him on the saddle as easily as he might handle a baby. Lassiter tried to kick him in the face. But Doane seized an ankle and twisted it so hard that Lassiter felt a stab of pain shoot up his leg. At first he thought the powerful twisting motion might have snapped a bone. But after a moment the throbbing pain subsided and he could move his foot.

"You can't get away with this, Sanlee!" Lassiter shouted. Someone had taken his rifle out of the saddle boot. With his revolver gone, all he had left were his fists, which he waved in the air for emphasis. "The sheriff will—"

Sanlee cut it off with a bellow of laughter. "I'm the sheriff here, Lassiter." Grinning through his beard, he took a badge from his pocket. He pinned it to the front of his faded work shirt: DEPUTY SHERIFF, TIEMPO COUNTY.

"An' I got here a legal posse," Sanlee continued with a sweep of his long arm. "Every man is deputized by *me!*"

"That's not legal." Lassiter was clutching at straws. "A sheriff has to do it."

"Why, damn me, you just might be right." Sanlee laughed. "But by the time we argue it out, you'll be in the ground."

Holding Millie in the vise of one arm, Sanlee pulled out a bandanna as Millie began to screech at him again, sobbing. While two of his men gripped the struggling Millie by the arms, Sanlee gagged her. Then he bound her wrists with a length cut from a catch rope. He walked her down the steps and to the buckboard that had just pulled up, boosting her onto the seat of it. One of the men sprang up beside her and gathered in the reins.

"Four of you go along with her," Sanlee said as he leveled a finger at them. "If any one of you puts a hand on her, that man is *dead.*" The warning was given quietly. But the men assigned to escort her to Diamond Eight were obviously impressed.

"Mrs. Dowd can handle her easy enough, once you get her home," Sanlee said. "Now clear out."

As the buckboard team sprang forward, hitting their collars, Millie turned her tear-stained face to Lassiter. Only for an instant did their eyes meet. Then he lost sight of her in the trees. Dust raised by the team and wagon and escorting riders drifted above the trees. . . .

Esperanza Herrera, who had remained out of sight during the invasion of the Diamond Eight men, made the sign of the cross when they pulled out. With her heart pounding, she hurried to the bedroom. She had to have riding clothes and she had none. So she exchanged her dress for a pair of her husband's trousers. They were too tight around the middle and she had to roll up the legs. And one of his shirts was too long. She tied the ends of it around her waist. Then she saddled a horse and started east to try and find her husband and the other men.

As she rode fast through the thickening heat, her lips murmured desperate prayers. The town of Santos was not too far and it was named for saints. Perhaps one of them would be nearby and hear her plea. She spurred the horse in a dead run toward the western boundary of Marcus Kilhaven's ranch. It was where her husband, Luis, had taken the crew. She prayed she would arrive in time. Poor Señor Lassiter was in the hands of the enemy. . . .

23

Pete Barkley riding a few yards ahead of the lead horseman shouted back to Sanlee. "Somebody's comin'!"

"Watch it," Sanlee warned tensely to his men and peered ahead through the screen of brush. It was where the road made a sweeping curve.

Lassiter, flanked by Diamond Eight men, tensed in the saddle of his black horse. From the corner of his eye, he studied the nearest man, calculating how far he would have to reach in order to seize a holstered gun. The man to his left was slightly nearer, but it would mean having to twist in the saddle so his right hand would be within range. But in shifting his gaze, he saw that the man on his right presented a solution. He was Jake Semple, obviously left-handed for his gun was worn on that side. All Lassiter had to do was lean in the saddle, snap out his right hand, while holding the reins in his left, and close his fingers over the butt.

As he tensed for the reckless gamble, however,

Semple pulled aside and out of reach. Every one of them was staring ahead to try and make out the rider Barkley had spotted. They could hear the sounds of an approaching horse.

Lassiter swore under his breath and settled back to wait for Semple to come again within reach. He rubbed the moist palm of his right hand along the seam of his canvas work pants. So far, they hadn't bound his wrists. One of the men had suggested it, but Sanlee said no. He had jeered at Lassiter, saying, "I wanta make it mighty temptin' for you to try an' get away. An' if you do, my boys got orders to shoot your legs out from under. That'll leave you alive. But before it's over you'll wish to Christ it had been quick."

"Murder in cold blood is what it adds up to."

"Naw, not at all. Hell, you tried to escape an' me an' my men bein' reps of the law, we had to cut you down. An' if you're beat all to hell an' bloodied up, we'll say you put up one hell of a fight. You get it, amigo?"

That was twenty minutes or so ago; Lassiter had lost all track of time. He had ridden in silence since then, his mind in turmoil for a time. Then he began coolly to turn over plan after plan, discarding each as too risky. But he knew there would come a time, and soon, when he would have to take the risk and to hell with the consequences.

He wondered who Pete Barkley had spotted up ahead. And he noticed how tense Sanlee and the men had become as they waited for the rider to appear. It made Lassiter think that Sanlee might not be quite as sure of himself as he pretended.

Isobel Hartney appeared suddenly around the bend in the road.

A broad grin followed a look of surprise on Sanlee's bearded face. "Why, howdy, ma'am," he sang out and his hat came off, his men baring their heads. "What're you doin' out this way?" Sanlee asked affably but with a definite note of strain in his voice.

For an answer she threaded her way through the staring Diamond Eight men and rode up to Lassiter. "I see I'm a little late," she said evenly. "They've already got you."

"Seems like," Lassiter said, looking deep into her green eyes, wondering just how much help she might be to him in this dangerous situation.

Isobel turned in the saddle. "Brad, I want you to turn him loose."

"Loose?" Sanlee's coarse brows shot up in mock surprise. "He ain't tied."

"Then you're free to ride away, Lassiter," she said. "We'll ride together."

Sanlee lost his patience. He swore and rode up to where she sat in her saddle. "Think again," he snarled. He leaned in the saddle toward her face, which seemed to have been carved out of white marble.

"I demand that you let him go!" she cried.

"Long as you seem to be hornin' in, Isobel honey, you can stay around an' watch me hang him!" He bit off the last few words and his lips twisted.

A tremor crossed her shoulders. "Your ridiculous story about Doc Clayburn . . ."

"There's some cottonwoods about a mile ahead. We'll find a good stout limb that'll hold his weight."

"I repeat, your ridiculous story that Doc Clayburn saw—"

It was as far as she got before Sanlee seized her by a wrist, twisting it so hard that she cried out. "Once we're hitched," he said in low-voiced fury, "you'll learn to keep your nose outta my business." He turned her loose and put on his hat. "Now you just ride along with us like a good little gal until we find us a good stout tree limb. This damn mesquite ain't worth a hang when it comes to hangin' a man." He laughed at his witticism.

"You're cruel and you're a monster," she said coldly.

"Yeah, ain't I both of 'em."

He threw back his head and began to laugh. His men, clapping hats back on their heads, joined in. The boss seemed in a good mood again, they were thinking, and the day held promise after all. It would be something to watch her face while Lassiter was kicking his life away at the end of a rope. Some of them wondered if she'd faint. A lot of women couldn't stand a hanging. Others could. Those who had known her for some years thought at times she had ice in her veins. She might get a little pale around the edges all right, but she'd watch the whole grim business with nary a whimper. But the fool woman didn't know enough to keep her mouth shut. She kept on arguing with the boss.

"Look at it this way, Brad. As long as you're a deputy sheriff with the power of arrest, and you say you have Doc Clayburn as a witness, why not do it the legal way? Let him have a fair trial."

"'Cause I figure to do it my way. He's cost me too much already. Besides that, I hear he's cheated the hangman a couple o' times already. Well, he ain't gonna cheat this one."

But finally he turned on her when she persisted in her argument. "Get back to town, pronto!" He glared. "I'll only tell you once. Give me any more trouble an' so help me, I'll pull you across my lap an' use the flat of my hand where you sit down. I'll do it right in front of *everybody!*"

She gave a deep sigh and her shoulders were slumped. There was defeat showing in her green eyes as she cast an imploring look at Lassiter. Then she turned her horse and galloped off through the brush.

Sanlee, in a shaking voice, said, "Let's find that goddamned tree!"

"I say you better tie the bastard," Shorty Doane spoke up.

Sanlee nodded. "Yeah, you're right, Shorty."

That was as far as he got. Jake Semple, the man on Lassiter's right, the left-landed one, big and tough-looking, had bumped his horse inadvertently against Lassiter's mount.

Lassiter leaned in the saddle just enough. His right hand shot out, his fingers closing over the gleaming, ivory butt of a .45. He cocked and aimed straight at Sanlee's broad back, no more than four feet away. Sanlee was still hunched in the saddle, staring at the spot where Isobel Hartney had disappeared. The sounds of her horse could still be faintly heard. He seemed to be on the verge of going after her, to bring her back and force her to witness the grim business after all. The whole move on Lassiter's part had used up no more time than a man taking a deep breath. The metallic click of the revolver being cocked seemed loud as a gong in the stillness.

"Anybody make a move," Lassiter sang out, "and Sanlee gets it right between the shoulder blades!"

Everyone stiffened. Sanlee looked over his shoulder, obeying Lassiter's warning to make no overt move. He stared at the barrel of the revolver as if it were a cave inhabited by ferocious bears.

"Throw down your guns, every one of you," Lassiter ordered crisply without a trace of fear or tension in his voice. But inwardly he was wound tight as a spring near the breaking point. "We're riding to town, you an' me, Sanlee. We're goin' to see Doc Clayburn. We're getting this witness business straightened out. Then you an' me . . . we're gonna face up to each other. And the best man will win. That'll be *me!*"

Sanlee, his head still twisted around in the awkward position of staring back, saw death in the cold blue eyes. He nodded his head. "Do what he says about the guns." Sanlee's voice was tight.

As everyone stared, Lassiter slowly urged his horse forward until he was within touching distance of Sanlee. Any one of them could have shot him in the back, Pinto George thought. But they knew he wasn't bluffing. Sanlee would die. And then his damn half-sister, Millie Chandler, would likely take over Diamond Eight and they'd be working for a female. Gad!

It was better to go along with what Lassiter wanted for now. Something would turn up. There was just too many of them and only one Lassiter.

Sanlee seemed to voice George's thoughts. "Don't take a chance," Sanlee told his men. "He means what he says."

Lassiter had them drop their revolvers and rifles onto the road. Still keeping his gun trained on Sanlee's back, he ordered Pinto George to run a catch rope through all the trigger guards. And when it was done, George handed up the doubled catch rope with its burden of weapons to Lassiter.

"Get moving," Lassiter ordered Sanlee. "But slowly. You try a wrong move and you'll be a bloody bundle of rags in the road."

Sanlee nodded that he understood, then started his horse at a walk with Lassiter keeping pace. Lassiter's right arm and hand seemed as rigid and unyielding as the steel of the weapon that could shatter Sanlee's spine. He had looped the reins over the saddle horn and was guiding the black horse with his knee pressure. In his left hand he gripped the ends of the catch rope that held the weapons taken from the Diamond Eight men. The men were some distance back down the road, sitting in their saddles, staring at their guns being dragged at the end of the rope, digging into the dirt and sending up a small cloud of dust.

Shorty Doane did not share the majority viewpoint that if they just sat tight, they'd get their guns back and finish Lassiter. Watching his chance, saying nothing to the others, he suddenly cut away from the road and was quickly swallowed up in the brush.

Although Lassiter heard the sudden movement, he didn't shift his aim to the fleeing Doane. It would give Sanlee and the others a split second in which to act.

Twenty minutes passed agonizingly slow. Sanlee still rode ahead, his big body tense, the unwavering .45 trained on his back. In Lassiter's wake, still generating a cloud of dust, were the captured guns, dragging at the end of the long rope.

Finally, Lassiter looked back where the road straightened out after a series of turns that the natives called the snake tracks. There was no sign of the Diamond Eight bunch. But he sensed they were back in the brush, hoping for a chance to get their hands on the weapons. A thin smile touched Lassiter's lips. He decided the weapons had been dragged far enough in loose dirt and sand.

"Hold it, Sanlee," he ordered. And when Sanlee halted, Lassiter swung the heavy burden at the end of the rope far off the road and into clumps of tornillo.

When they were moving again, still at a walk, Sanlee cleared his throat. "I got a deal for you, Lassiter."

"I remember your first deal—a list of three men you wanted dead." Lassiter's laughter was harsh.

"I figured you were just a cold-blooded killer an' would jump at it. That's what some folks claim about you, anyhow. Listen, here's what I got in mind. You turn me loose an' head out of Texas. I'll send you $10,000. All you got to do is name the bank."

"You oughta be a tent-show comedian."

"I ain't foolin', Lassiter. I'll write out an agreement an' make it legal."

"Yeah. And tonight every star will fall out of the sky."

"I swear, Lassiter. . . ."

"Sanlee, we both know it's gone too far for that."

"With $10,000, you can loaf an' not do one damn thing."

"Vince Tevis was my friend. Ten thousand won't buy back his life."

"I never killed him."

"Maybe, maybe not. But you hired the men who did." Lassiter stared at the back of Sanlee's neck and the short, reddish hairs that curled against the sweated skin.

"When we face up, I'll be doing my damnedest to

kill you," Lassiter said. "As you'll be trying to do to me."

"All right, Lassiter, you won't listen about the money, so maybe you'll listen to this. Sheriff Palmer is mighty close to the Texas Rangers. You push on with this idea of yours an' those boys'll be on your tail. They never give up."

"And neither do you, it seems like. Now shut up till we get to town."

"If I could trust you to give me a fair shake, I know I can take you."

"You'll get a fair shake."

"No tricks?"

"None."

Sanlee laughed. "If a fella shook you real hard, your brain would rattle like a dried pea. An' just as big, too. You're short on what's supposed to be upstairs in your head."

"I told you to shut up."

Somehow he'd have to fill Sanlee's empty holster. He supposed he should have kept one of the revolvers taken from the Diamond Eight men. But he hadn't, and it was too late now. Perhaps Doc Clayburn had a spare gun. As for the .45 Lassiter kept trained on Sanlee's back, it was heavier than the weapon he was used to, his .44. But it had been taken along with his rifle back at Box C. So he had to forget it for the present.

The sun beat down through a rift in boiling clouds. A slight wind sent sand shushing against mesquite trunks.

Lassiter knew he'd have to make do with the gun he'd snatched from Semple. That he had been able to pull it off was a miracle. He had simply caught everyone by surprise. He was nearing town now and left the road for a trail through the undergrowth.

Finally, through towering brush and cottonwoods, Lassiter glimpsed the roof line of a two-story building where Doc Clayburn lived and had his office. He forced Sanlee to ride along the east side of the building, which was some distance from the main part of town. No one seemed to be around. Had all the pressure Sanlee had been putting on him caused the doctor to flee from Santos? But when they came around to the street side, Lassiter breathed easier. The door to the doctor's office in the narrow building was wide open. . . .

At Diamond Eight, Mrs. Elva Dowd stared at Millie Chandler, her wrists bound, who had been shoved through the doorway by two of the men. "The boss says for you to keep an eye on his sister an' hold her here till he gets back," one of the men said.

"Where is he?"

"In town by now, I reckon. He's got Lassiter." He didn't add that if Sanlee had brought Lassiter to town, it was probably as a dead body.

Elva Dowd grunted something and closed the door on the two men. "What do I do with you?" the woman asked heavily as she turned to Millie.

"Untie me!" Millie twisted around and thrust her bound wrists at the austere housekeeper. The woman thought about it.

"You gotta promise you won't try an' skeedaddle."

"These ropes are hurting me. Please, Mrs. Dowd. *Please!*"

Mrs. Dowd studied the young widow's stricken face, weighing it against her brother Brad's displeasure if something went wrong. She reluctantly untied her wrists.

Rubbing at indentations left in her flesh by the rope, Millie hurried to a front window. She could see the buckboard team tied to the corral fence in the distance. The men were too lazy to put it up, at least for now. They were in the bunkhouse, no doubt, having a pull at a bottle and talking over the experience of the day.

But when she wheeled for the front door, Mrs. Dowd sprang forward and grabbed her by an arm. With her superior height and weight, the woman held Millie easily in her grasp.

"You promised," the woman reminded thinly.

"Let me go!" Millie cried. In desperation, she swung a fist that landed solidly on the woman's jaw. The eyes of Elva Dowd were suddenly crossed. She slumped to the floor in a tangle of skirts and petticoats.

Then Millie ran as quietly as she could all the way to the corral, stepping in the thick dust so her footfalls would be minimized. She kept the buckboard team to a walk until clear of the house, then she slapped the reins along their backs and shouted at them. They lunged into a gallop, hauling the buckboard at a dangerous speed along the rough ranch road. . . .

24

At the east side of Doc Clayburn's building, Lassiter, still keeping a gun trained on Sanlee, ordered him to dismount.

"Tie the horses," Lassiter ordered brusquely.

Sanlee scowled, but obeyed. Then Lassiter forced him to walk very slowly, his hands raised shoulder high, around to the street and the front entrance to the medical office.

A plump Mexican woman was sitting on a stool discussing some problem with the doctor. When Sanlee and Lassiter entered the office, a look of fear touched her plump dark face at sight of the drawn gun.

"We're not going to hurt you, señora," Lassiter said softly in Spanish. "Leave now, if you will. You can see the doctor later."

She scurried out of the building, not looking back. Doc Clayburn, looking unutterably weary, sank to the stool so recently occupied by the woman. "What's your next move, Lassiter? Kill us both?"

"I want you to write out the truth, Doc. You didn't

see me murder Buck Rooney. You weren't anywhere near the spot where he was killed that day."

"And if I refuse?"

Sanlee, who had been glaring at the doctor, now relaxed and a faint smile appeared on his bearded lips. Sweat showed through the coarse, reddish hair where his hat was tipped back. He started to lower his hands, but Lassiter jabbed him in the back with the gun barrel. He lifted them again.

"I think you're a fair man, Doc," Lassiter said. "An honest man. Sanlee has some hold over you. I don't know what it is. You tell me."

Sanlee gave a short laugh. "I offered Lassiter $10,000 to clear out. Can you figure him turnin' it down, Doc? An' now he's got you to point the finger at him for killin' Rooney. Maybe Lassiter don't know it, but he's already got one foot on the gallows' steps."

"You don't have to be afraid of Sanlee," Lassiter said patiently to Doc Clayburn. "Because after you tell the truth about Rooney, I figure to blow him outta his boots."

"Back in New York a man was seeing my wife. I caught him. We shot it out. I was the lucky one and he was dead. But the man had powerful friends. I had to run."

"Pick up a pen and write what you just told me—and the rest of it," Lassiter said over Sanlee's shoulder.

"Maybe I should go back to New York and face up to it after all these years." Doc Clayburn gave Sanlee a tired smile. "What do you think, Brad?"

"Doc, you better not even think about it," Sanlee said coldly. But there was an edge of worry in the voice. Lassiter carefully stepped around Sanlee so he could see the man's eyes. There was a definite wariness in the gray depths. Lassiter smiled.

"Doc, will you tell the truth about Rooney?" Lassiter asked the man slumped on the stool. "If you shot that man in a fair fight . . ."

"I did."

"Then your conscience is clear."

"But there are others to consider—my daughter, my grandchildren." Clayburn looked up. There were hollows under his eyes and his mouth sagged. "I can't do it, Lassiter."

"Don't tell me I figured you wrong, Doc," Lassiter said quietly.

"Lassiter, you've got a chance. Take it and get out." Clayburn's voice shook. "You can't stand up against Diamond Eight. Nobody can. Brad Sanlee has got this county sewed up in his own private bag. Go ahead. You've got a weapon. Sanlee is unarmed. It's your one chance."

"You heard him, Lassiter," Sanlee said with a laugh.

Lassiter said, "All right, if Doc won't help me, then I've only got you. I can start on you, Sanlee, and work my way up till you shout the truth about Buck Rooney. Shout it loud enough so they can hear you all the way uptown!"

"What'd you mean when you said work your way up?" Sanlee demanded suspiciously, his tongue tip snaking through the beard to lick his lower lip.

"It means I'll start at the kneecap. If a bullet there doesn't loosen your tongue, then I'll bust a hip bone. Next a couple of ribs. I think about then you'll scream to high heaven that I didn't have one damn thing to do with killin' Buck Rooney."

"You ain't the kind to do that to a man," Sanlee sneered. But it failed to carry to the gray eyes.

Lassiter stared hard at his captive, then finally gave a short laugh. "I reckon maybe you're right, Sanlee. Doc, have you got a spare gun?"

Clayburn looked up with a frown. "I have, but . . ."

"Give it to Sanlee," he said in a hard voice. "Then the two of us will step into the street. And only one of us will walk away."

Clayburn thought about it for a moment, then got up from the stool and stumbled over to a desk. He reached for a drawer, which drew a warning from Lassiter. "Careful, Doc. Just open it real easy. No tricks."

Clayburn nodded. His hand shook so that the drawer rattled when he opened it. Reaching in, he withdrew a .45-caliber gun with black grips, holding it by the barrel so the tall man with the cold blue eyes wouldn't misjudge his intent. The weapon thumped against the desk top as he laid it down.

At that moment, riders suddenly appeared in the street in front of the building, the brown dust from their horses billowing against the clearing sky. Lassiter looked out to see Luis Herrera and his vaqueros dismounting. Herrera bounded into the doctor's office, his white teeth gleaming under his mustache.

"Señora Aguilar, she tell me where you are, Lassiter!" Herrera said, referring to Doc Clayburn's recent patient. Then Herrera looked at Sanlee, white-faced and standing with his hands lifted. "Ah, you have defanged the snake," Herrera said in Spanish.

Five vaqueros, all the crew Box C had left, were staring at the tableau.

"My wife, she fetch us," Herrera was explaining to Lassiter as he brandished a carbine.

* * *

A few minutes earlier, five Diamond Eight men had come boiling into town by the back way and flung themselves from their horses and charged into the store.

Isobel Hartney, who had been cold with worry over Lassiter's fate, but knowing she was helpless to do anything about it, looked up to see Pinto George, Jeddy Quine, Pete Barkley, Joe Tige and Jake Semple come rushing through the store. Isobel had been showing new corsets to some of the ladies.

"We need guns!" Pinto George shouted at her.

"Just a minute, can't you see I'm busy?" A faint hope for Lassiter's safety flared in her. All along, she had told herself that Brad wouldn't dare hang him. You didn't arrest a man, then kill him as you were taking him to jail.

"We need guns *now!*" George yelled and moved toward a large glass showcase with a display of revolvers and rifles.

Isobel frowned but managed a show of indignation. The ladies looked frightened, suspecting the men were drunk.

"I refuse to be shouted at," Isobel said firmly.

Pinto George screamed, "Goddamn Lassiter took our guns and dragged 'em in sand. They ain't worth a damn till they're cleaned. We ain't got time for that. He's down at Doc's place. We seen him go in!"

He got behind the showcase and tried to slide open the wooden doors, but they were locked. "Gimme the key!"

"Get out of here!" Isobel cried. Her two white-faced clerks were huddled in fear and confusion.

Lassiter had outwitted the bunch of them. And as Isobel stood with Lassiter's roguish image flashing through her consciousness, Pinto George seized some tinned tomatoes and used the heavy can to start smashing in the top of her showcase. Glass shattered and shards tinkled to the floor. The ladies at the corset counter were terrified.

Pinto George and the others reached into the maw at the top of the showcase, snatching up revolvers and rifles. On a shelf in back of the gun case were boxes of cartridges, which they feverishly tore open, loading the weapons, stuffing spare shells into their pockets.

"Let's go get that son of a bitch!" Joe Tige yelled. He shuffled toward the door, bent over because of a bulky bandage that covered his chest.

Isobel Hartney emerged from her visions of Lassiter and rushed to the door ahead of Tige. She tried to block him. "Leave Lassiter alone!"

"He killed Rooney!"

"He *didn't!*" she screamed.

Joe Tige laughed in her face. By then, Pinto George, Barkley, Quine and Semple had swarmed up. They shoved her out of the way and streamed into the middle of the dusty street. Frightened faces peered at them from windows up and down the block. Far down the street, four vaqueros from Box C were standing rigidly in front of Doc Clayburn's building, which sat alone at the edge of Santos.

25

Since the moment the plump Señora Aguilar had fled the doctor's office, Lassiter had been aware that the ancient timbers of the former whorehouse were coming to life under the heat of a climbing sun. But now, suddenly, there was another creak, a deeper one as if a great weight crossed the floor in the rear part of the structure. Lassiter suddenly felt as if the door to an ice house had opened at his back. His head came up. It was at that moment that he first heard a great smashing of glass coming from farther uptown.

"What in the hell was that!" Herrera cried.

But Lassiter was looking over his shoulder at Shorty Doane. The big man stood in a doorway leading to a long, dim hallway with closed doors on either side, the former working and sleeping quarters of the givers of pleasure to range-land males. Because of his height, Doane had to stoop. He wore a broad grin on his scarred face. Some of the scars were old and others, more recent, resulted from the slashing fists of the man who stood half-turned, a gun in hand. The weapon was trained on a grim Brad Sanlee.

With Shorty Doane's sudden appearance in a rear doorway, hope flashed in Sanlee's gray eyes like a blinding beacon. For Shorty Doane was lifting the first weapon he had been able to get his hands on after he had deserted his companions to go it alone. No longer was there any possible execution of Doane's plan to make Lassiter's death as ugly as possible at the point of a knife. Now he wanted to get it over with!

In the space of seconds it had taken for Lassiter to realize the giant's ominous presence, Doane yelled, "Brad . . . *jump!*"

And Brad Sanlee did just that, hurling himself headfirst to an open window. As he was clearing it, Lassiter dropped hard to the floor, all thoughts of trying to bring Sanlee down erased from his mind. It was now self-preservation.

A roar rattled through the windows and shook the office. Smoke belched as buckshot screamed and dug splinters from walls and demolished a front window, the sheet of lead directed solely at the spot where Lassiter had been standing only a heartbeat before.

He felt a numbing along his back, a wetness. But in desperation he twisted to a supine position on the freshly scrubbed floor. He saw Doane still in the hall doorway. A row of yellow teeth were revealed as he lifted the shotgun to discharge the second barrel. But before the barrel settled on the intended target, Lassiter shot him. Doane's head snapped back and the shotgun roared again, this time sending that scythe of shot into the ceiling. Powdered plaster fell like a sheet of snow. Doane collapsed, still holding the shotgun, now empty.

Lassiter picked himself up, aware of a groaning sound, wondering dully if he was the source. Painfully he made his way to Doane. He was aware of shouting from farther uptown.

"Kill you," Doane breathed, staring up out of shocked eyes. "It's all I wanted. . . ." Then, as if punctured, the great bleeding chest collapsed and his head rolled to one side.

Lassiter turned around. The pain burned like the heated blades of a dozen knives. He saw Doc Clayburn lying on his back. Blood from several wounds formed a puddle. Breathing hard, Lassiter forced himself to walk over to where Herrera was crumpled in the doorway. The whole purpose of Lassiter's extensive maneuvering had been to save lives. And now it looked as if Hell's double doors had burst open to incinereate anyone within reach.

In front of the building, the vaqueros were firing at something down the street. Bullets slammed into the side of the building as they began to give ground. Rudy Ruiz made what appeared to be a grand bow, then he toppled and fell across his rifle in the rutted street.

"Lassiter's inside!" It was Sanlee's screech. *"Get him!"*

Jamming the .45 into his belt, Lassiter snatched up the carbine Herrera had dropped. At a crouching run, despite pain, he hopped over the crumpled segundo and reached the street. Those advancing from the Hartney Store missed a beat in surprise at Lassiter's boldness. His first shot doubled up Pinto George. His second knocked Jeddy Quine into a twisting gargoyle, blood streaming down his face.

Semple, the left-handed one, whirled like a dervish as a bullet crashed into his shoulder.

Shocked by Lassiter's sudden and devastating marksmanship, Joe Tige fired in haste, the bullet ricocheting off Doc Clayburn's metal sign above the door. By then the shot from Luis Herrera's carbine, now in the capable hands of a frenzied Lassiter, dug deep through the packed bandage on Tige's chest and out of his body.

Pete Barkley started to lift his rifle, then wheeled in panic. He threw away his weapon and started back up the street at a limping run, past spectators frozen along the walks or taking refuge in buildings. The blacksmith was crouched behind his cooling tank.

Black specks were whirling in front of Lassiter's eyes and his knees felt wobbly. He let Barkley go and started to turn. From a corner of his eye he saw Brad Sanlee snatch the gun from Pinto George's dead hand. For a big man, Sanlee seemed to have the speed of a gazelle as he sprinted for the safety of a building wall. In the next instant a bullet fired from Sanlee's weapon ripped the rifle out of Lassiter's hands. Lassiter felt a numbness to the tips of his fingers. The shock of the blow sent him stumbling to his knees. A second bullet whipped past the tip of his nose.

Far up the street he saw Isobel Hartney at a run from her store, her blond hair tumbling, skirts and apron flying. "Get back!" he yelled, gesturing with a numbed hand.

Added to that awful moment was the sudden appearance of Rep Chandler's widow. For some seconds, Lassiter had been aware of the growing sounds made by a fast-moving team and wagon. He watched in horror as Millie Chandler came whipping out of a side street in a buckboard. She was standing up, lashing a lathered team that ran as if their hindquarters were licked by flame, eyes wild, manes streaming. Millie's hair was a dark banner caught by the wind.

Her eyes were on Lassiter, on his knees, some distance down the street, as if in an attitude of prayer. Around him, three vaqueros were dragging themselves away. A fourth lay unmoving. Herrera was crumpled in the doorway. She came pounding past Isobel Hartney and on down the street, her buckboard skidding dangerously. Then she spotted Sanlee and made a slight shift with the reins. Sanlee saw her coming and turned his big body.

"Millie!" he screamed. In his eyes was a mixture of hatred and adoration.

As the speeding team and buckboard bore down, he leaped aside, for it was obvious that her intention was to run him down. But the left rear hub of the speeding wheel caught an awning post and ripped it out. The rear wheel went flying as did Millie, like a black-haired rag doll flung by an angry child.

The last Lassiter saw, she was tucking her body into a curl. And then a great cloud of dust erupted like a blinding midnight fog.

Hurt as he was, bleeding from a dozen or more shotgun wounds, Lassiter was barely able to fling himself away from the forefeet of the terrified team. On down the street they raced, the buckboard tilting unsteadily. A great geyser of dirt and dust was hurled into the air from the left rear axle that was digging into the street.

As the dust began to clear, Lassiter saw Sanlee step suddenly into view from a slot between buildings thirty feet away. The gun he had taken from Pinto George hung straight down his side.

"All right, you son of a bitch!" Sanlee screamed. His hat was gone and coarse, reddish hair hung down on either side of his face. "You killed my sister, as sure as if you shot her with a gun!" Tears streamed into his beard and ran through the rust-colored hairs to lips stretched across bared teeth.

Lassiter, sickened by what Sanlee had yelled about his sister, dug for the revolver he had thrust into his waistband. A bullet sliced across his right thigh like a hot iron. He stumbled and nearly went down.

Sanlee was lurching toward him, drawing back the hammer of his weapon for another shot. That was when Lassiter emptied the .45 he had jerked from Semple's holster. Sanlee's image was as if viewed through heat waves. But the blurred vision received at least two of the bullets; the rest smashed into the wooden parapet above the building, which had lost its awning pole. One end of the wooden awning sagged precariously.

"He's down!" a man shouted. "Sanlee's *down!*"

Men swarmed around Lassiter much as they had the day he had beaten Shorty Doane with his fists. Letting the empty gun slip from his fingers, he pushed through the growing crowd over to where he had seen Millie hurled into the street. She was sitting up, supporting a broken arm.

She looked up at him with a shocked, white face. "I tried my best to kill him. To kill my own brother." Then the tears sprang from her eyes in a flood. "Oh, Lassiter . . ." was all she could manage.

And when he turned to stumble over to where Sanlee lay at the edge of the street, she saw the bloodied back of his shirt and nearly fainted.

Sanlee was staring up. A man fanned him with a hat.

"Tell 'em about Buck Rooney," Lassiter said, breathing hard.

"Go to hell."

"I didn't kill him. You know damn well I didn't."

Sanlee was laughing when the light went out of his gray eyes and they stared, unblinking, up into the noonday sun directly overhead.

It was found that both Clayburn and Luis Herrera had received superficial but painful wounds from a peripheral buckshot that had exploded from Doane's shotgun. A bandaged Doc Clayburn gave instructions to Señora Herrera, who had come from Box C in a wagon and now was ready to take the wounded back to the ranch. One dead one, Rudy Ruiz, who had survived the ambush and stampede, had his luck run out in Santos.

Lassiter didn't go with the wagon. Isobel Hartney took charge of his care, putting him in her big bed above the store. Under the tragic circumstances, no one mentioned the moral implications of such an arrangement. Because of the wounds in his back, Lassiter was forced to sleep on his stomach. But one day he was able to turn over, which brought a smile of delight to the one who had been nursing him for a week.

"My darling," Isobel whispered. She started to take down her hair so that the sweet scent of it was in his nostrils. She whispered, "I've been thinking. We'll run the store together. It'll be yours as well as mine."

But he regretfully pushed her away and had a long talk. And when he had finished, she said bitterly, "It's Millie Chandler, isn't it?"

He shook his head. And that gave her some satisfaction.

That day he rode out to Box C. It seemed that a hundred miles had somehow been added to the trip. When he arrived, he was exhausted. Luis Herrera was sitting in a chair outside his small house, looking wan. He waved and Lassiter waved back. He found Millie sitting on the sofa, the bandage of her splinted arm only slightly whiter than her face. "I see you pried yourself away from Lady Bountiful."

"How are you feeling, Millie?"

"Like hell." Tears sparkled in her eyes. "How else? Without you."

He sat beside her on the sofa in silence for a few moments while he got his breath after the ride. He stared at the maw of the big stone fireplace. Somehow it reminded him of his own future—dark and without purpose. Then he flung aside the feeling of depression. He couldn't help the way he was built. As he had once told Rep Chandler: "To see what's on the other side of the mountain."

"I heard what you told the sheriff," Millie said. "That Doc had been in some trouble back East and that you wondered if Brad had ever said anything about it. And when the sheriff said he hadn't, you said something about letting sleeping dogs lie, that it hadn't been Doc's fault, the old killing. And the new killing couldn't be blamed on you. Buck Rooney. You spoke right up to the sheriff."

"I did."

"And Sheriff Palmer was in his best baby-kissing, electioneering mood because you had reminded him that I, as Brad Sanlee's only living relative, would take over his ranch. And that Diamond Eight in addition to Box C would make me a power in Tiempo County."

"So I did." He gave her a rueful smile.

"Damn it, Lassiter, I'd trade it all. . . . If only you were different. I don't know how many times you've told me that you're a drifter, that you can't stay in one place very long. . . ." Her voice was shaking.

"Listen, I've been thinking. Marcus Kilhaven . . ."

"Oh, yes. Brad had spoken to him about me. I was to be bartered again as I was with poor old Rep. But Marcus said he told Brad right out that he didn't want me that way, that I had to want him for himself. Not just to please my . . . my brother." She put a hand to her eyes. "Brad's dead and the horror is finished. But, my God, at what a price. The dead, the wounded . . ."

"I wanted it to be just between the two of us—Brad an' me. But it didn't quite turn out that way." He gave a deep sigh. "I better get over to my own quarters. . . ."

"Stay the night, Lassiter. I want to argue against your leaving." She bit her lips and tried to smile. "And I just might win out in the end."

But she didn't. He rode out one midnight. He had left her a long note. One thing he dreaded was a tearful good-bye. But he would always remember the Santos country and the price of avenging the death of his friend, Vince Tevis, and of leaving behind two beautiful women. It would have been damned hard, had he been so inclined, to choose between them. But now he didn't have to. His nature as a drifter was too strong.

BLOOD TRAIL TO KANSAS

ROBERT J. RANDISI

Ted Shea thinks he is a goner for sure. All the years he's worked to build his Montana spread and fine herd of prime beef means nothing if he can't sell them. And with a vicious rustler and his gang of cutthroats scaring all the hands, no one is willing to take to the trail. Until Dan Parmalee drifts into town. A gunman and gambler with a taste for long odds, he isn't about to let a little hot lead part him from some cold cash. But it doesn't take Dan long to realize this isn't just any run. This is a...*Blood Trail to Kansas*.

ISBN 10: 0-8439-5799-9
ISBN 13: 978-0-8439-5799-0 $5.99 US/$7.99 CAN
